HEARTBREAK TANGO

Manuel Puig was born in 1932 in a small town in the Argentine pampas. He studied philosophy at the University of Buenos Aires, and in 1956 won a scholarship from the Italian Institute in Buenos Aires and chose to pursue studies in film direction at the Cinecitta in Rome. There he worked in films until 1962, when he began to write his first novel. Exiled from Argentina, he settled in New York City in 1963. Puig's novels – BETRAYED BY RITA HAYWORTH, HEARTBREAK TANGO, THE BUENOS AIRES AFFAIR, KISS OF THE SPIDER WOMAN, and ETERNAL CURSE ON THE READER OF THESE PAGES – have been translated into fourteen languages and secured his brilliant international reputation.

A master of style and invention, and a provocative and compassionate thinker, Manuel Puig is one of the best known and one of the most original of the 'second generation' of Latin American writers. In that context, his work is perhaps most significant for breaking with the metaphysical or allegorical bent of writers like Borges, Cortázar, Fuentes and García Márquez. Puig's main concern is personal relationships and the cultural context in which they exist. Keenly aware of how both the novel and the people who are its best subjects have been swept up in the clichés of popular culture and ideologies, Puig, like Nabokov, takes constant delight in the trashier aspects of contemporary culture, while turning it against itself to illustrate how it warps both lives and dreams through his immense irony and wit. The earlier novels, especially, use humour and satire to reveal the insidious but brutal cultural imp_____ __ _____ the United States has sub-

ALSO IN ARENA BY MANUEL PUIG

Betrayed by Rita Hayworth
Eternal Curse On the Reader of These Pages
Kiss of the Spider Woman

Manuel Puig

HEARTBREAK TANGO
A Serial

Translated by Suzanne Jill Levine

An Arena Book

Published by Arrow Books Limited
62–65 Chandos Place, London WC2N 4NW

An imprint of Century Hutchinson Limited

London Melbourne Sydney Auckland
Johannesburg and agencies throughout
the world

First published in Great Britain 1987

Printed and bound in Great Britain by
The Guernsey Press Co. Ltd,
Guernsey, C.I.

ISBN 0 09 940530 X

HEARTBREAK TANGO

A tango lingers on true red lips

FIRST EPISODE

The shadows on the dance floor,
this tango brings sad memories to mind,
let us dance and think no more
while my satin dress
like a tear shines.

(from H. Manzi's tango "His Voice")

NOTICE APPEARING IN THE APRIL 1947 EDITION OF THE MONTHLY PUBLICATION "OUR NEIGHBORHOOD," PRINTED IN THE TOWN OF VALLEJOS, PROVINCE OF BUENOS AIRES

"LAMENTED BEREAVEMENT. The untimely passing of Juan Carlos Etchepare on the 18th of April last, at the early age of twenty-nine, after suffering a long and distressing illness, has produced in the people of this town, of which the deceased was a beloved son, a profound sentiment of sorrowful dismay, notwithstanding the fact that many close friends knew of the serious disease with which the late lamented was afflicted.

This demise marks the loss of an element from our midst which, for his remarkable spirit and integrity, stood out among us as a human being of great worth, possessing as he did either vast attributes or gifts, such as his personal charm, which either distinguish or set apart those who possess this immeasurable wealth and who therefore earn the admiration, deference, or affection of either friends or strangers.

The remains of Juan Carlos Etchepare were interred in the local burial ground, accompanied to their final home by a grief-stricken funeral cortege."

My Dear Mrs. Etchepare:

I learned of the sad news from "Our Neighborhood" and after many doubts I got up the courage to send you my most heartfelt condolences on the death of your son.

I am Nélida Fernández de Massa, they used to call me Nené, remember? I've been living in Buenos Aires for several years now, soon after I got married I came to live here with my husband, but this terrible news made me decide to drop you a few lines despite the fact that before my marriage yourself and your daughter Celina had stopped speaking to me. In spite of everything poor Juan Carlos always said hello to me, may he rest in peace! The last time I saw him was nine years ago.

I don't know if you still hold a grudge against me, Mrs. Etchepare, but in any case I sincerely hope the good Lord is with you in this hour of need, it must be hard to resign oneself to such a loss, a son already a full-grown man.

In spite of the three hundred and two miles that separate Buenos Aires from Vallejos, I am by your side in this moment. Even though you may not wish it, let me pray with you.

Nélida Fernández de Massa

Under the new fluorescent light in the kitchen, she looks at her hands after closing the ink bottle, and noticing that the fingers which held the pen are stained, she goes to the sink to wash them off. With a stone she removes the ink and dries her hands with a dishtowel. She takes the envelope, wets the gummed edge with saliva and looks for a few seconds at the multicolored rhombuses on the oilcloth which covers the table.

*

Dear Mrs. Etchepare:

What a relief when I got your letter! The truth is I didn't expect it, I thought you would never forgive me. On the other hand I see that your daughter Celina still looks down upon me, and I will write to your post office box as you ask, so that you won't have arguments with her. You know what I thought when I saw your envelope? I thought that inside would be my unopened letter.

Mrs. Etchepare . . . I feel so sad, I know I shouldn't be telling you this, it's me who should be comforting you. But how can I explain, there's just nobody I can talk to about Juan Carlos, and all day long I keep thinking that such a young and good-looking boy had to have the misfortune of catching that disease. I often wake up at night and without wanting to I start thinking about Juan Carlos.

I knew that he was sick, that he had gone to the Cordoban Mountains to get better, but I don't know why . . . somehow I didn't feel sorry for him, or maybe I just couldn't believe that he could possibly die. Now I can only think of one thing since he never went to church, did he confess before dying? I hope to God he did, it's one more relief for those of us who remain after him, don't you think so? It's been quite a while since I last prayed, three years ago when my younger son was unwell, but now I've started praying again. Another thing I'm afraid of is that he might have gone through with what he wanted. Did he ever tell you? I hope to God he didn't! You see, Mrs. Etchepare, that too comes to my mind when I wake up at night: it so happens that Juan Carlos told me more than once that when he died he wanted to be cremated. It seems to me that the Catholic church disapproves of this, because the catechism says that after Judgment Day will come the resurrection of the body and the soul. Now I don't go to confession these days since I got out of the habit years ago, but I am going to ask some Father about that. Yes, Mrs. Etchepare, of course Juan Carlos is resting, it suddenly came to me that at least he is resting, if not yet in Heaven. Oh yes, of that we can be sure, because Juan Carlos never hurt a soul. Well, I look forward to hearing from you soon.

Affectionately,
Nélida

In a drawer next to the child's rosary, first communion veil, and pictures of saints in the name of the child Alberto Luis Massa, there is a book covered in imitation mother-of-pearl. She leafs through it until she comes to a passage that predicts Judgment Day and the resurrection of the flesh.

*

Buenos Aires, June 10, 1947

Dear Mrs. Etchepare:

This afternoon when I came back from shopping downtown for some things for the boys, I found your letter. I felt a great relief in knowing that Juan Carlos confessed before dying and had a Christian burial. All considered it's a great comfort. And how are you doing? are you feeling a little cheerier? I'm still so down in the mouth.

Now you may find this uncalled-for, but when he went away to Córdoba the first time, he wrote quite a few love letters to me in Vallejos. He said things that I never forgot, which I shouldn't say because I'm a married woman now with two healthy children, two sons, one eight and the other six, God bless them, and I shouldn't be thinking about things years ago, but when I wake up at night I always think what a comfort it would be to reread the letters Juan Carlos wrote to me. When we stopped speaking to each other, and after what happened with Celina, we sent back the letters. It wasn't that we had an argument, it was just that one day I suddenly received all my letters by mail, the ones I had sent him in Córdoba, so then I returned all the ones he had written to me. He might have burned them, I don't know, maybe not . . . I had them tied in a sky-blue ribbon, because they were a boy's letters, he returned mine lumped together in a big envelope, and you should have seen how mad I got because they weren't tied in a pink ribbon as I had asked him when we were still on speaking terms, what things a girl would make a fuss about at that age. Those were the days.

Who knows if those letters are still around. If you yourself found them would you burn them? What are you folks planning to do with all those things of Juan Carlos's that are personal? I know that he once kept another girl's handkerchief with rouge on it, he told me so to get me all worked up. Then I wondered that if you didn't mind and you happened to find those letters he wrote me, that maybe you could send them to me.

Well, Mrs. Etchepare, I hope you'll keep writing to me, one thing that surprised me was your steady handwriting, it seems like a young person's, good for you, and to think that you suffered such a great misfortune lately. You don't have someone else write them for you, do you?

Remember that my letters are the ones in the sky-blue ribbon, that's enough to know which ones, because they don't have envelopes, when I kept them I was silly and threw away the envelopes, because I felt that they had been handled by other people, don't you think I was right in a way? In the post office many hands touch the envelopes, but only Juan Carlos, poor boy, touched the page inside, and then me, only us two, so the page inside really is an intimate thing. So now you know by the pretty blue ribbon, you don't have to read the heading to know which letters are mine.

Well, Mrs. Etchepare, I hope these words find you in better spirits.

Yours most affectionately,
Nené

She closes the envelope, turns on the radio, and starts to change out of old house clothes into a street dress. The program "Tango Versus Bolero" has just begun. A tango and a bolero are alternately played. The tango relates the misfortune of a man who in the winter rain remembers the warm moonlit night when he met his beloved and the following rainy night when he lost her, expressing his fear that the next day the sun will come out and not even then will she return to his side, a possible sign of her death. He finally asks that if she does not return, then neither should the geraniums in the patio blossom if its petals will only wither soon after. Next, the bolero describes a couple's separation despite their love for each other, a separation determined by secret reasons of his own: he cannot tell her the reason and asks her to believe that he will return if circumstances permit, as the fishing boat returns to its moorings if the storms in the Caribbean Sea do not wreck it. The program closes. In front of the mirror in which she continues looking at herself, after putting on lipstick and powdering her face, she gathers up her hair in an attempt to recreate a hairdo in vogue several years back.

*

Buenos Aires, June 22, 1947

Dear Mrs. Etchepare:

I was just about to write without waiting for an answer when your nice little letter fortunately arrived. I am happy to know that things are easier now that you have less visitors, people mean well but don't realize that they're a bother when there are so many of them.

I was just about to write because in the last letter I forgot to ask you if Juan Carlos is buried in the ground, in a niche, or in some family mausoleum. I so much hope that he's not in the ground. . . . Did you ever get into a pit that someone was digging? Because then if you put your hand against the hard dirt in the hole you feel how cold and damp it is, with rocks, sharp pieces, and where the dirt is soft it's worse yet, because that's where the worms are. I'm not sure if those are the worms who later look for what for them is nutrition, better left unsaid, I don't know how they can get into such a thick and hard wooden box. Unless after many years the box rots away and they can get in, but then I don't know why boxes aren't made out of iron or steel. But now that I think of it I remember that it also seems that we carry the worms inside, I think I read that somewhere, that when medical students have their classes in the morgue they see the worms when they cut up the corpse, I'm not sure if I read it or if someone told me so. It's much better for him to be in a niche, although you can't put a lot of flowers there all on the same occasion, I also prefer that to being in a beautiful mausoleum, if it's not his own family's, because it would seem like they were doing him a favor. Oh, now I remember who told me that awful thing about us carrying the worms inside ourselves, it was Juan Carlos himself, that's why he wanted to be cremated, so that the worms wouldn't eat him. Forgive me if this upsets you, but who can I talk to about these memories if not with you?

What I'm not sure about is how to explain how Juan Carlos's letters began. How strange they don't have the pretty blue ribbon anymore. Did you find that many letters? How strange, Juan Carlos swore to me that it was the first time he ever wrote to a girl, of course after that the years passed, but what use were the letters if we broke up just the same, so that's why silly me got it into my head that he was dead set against the idea of corresponding with a girl. Just an idea I had, that's all.

The letters addressed to me were all written on the same paper which I bought for him along with a fountain pen when he went away to Córdoba. It's a kind of white paper with little wrinkles that almost seems like raw silk. The heading changes sometimes, he wouldn't use my name because he said it was compromising in case my mother found them I could say they were letters for another girl. The main thing I think is that they're dated from July to September 1937, and if you happen to read a bit, Mrs. Etchepare, don't go and believe everything he says, that was Juan Carlos for you, he liked to get me all worked up.

Please try as hard as you can to find them and thank you so much for sending them to me.

As ever,
Nené

She hasn't addressed the envelope yet, she stands up abruptly, leaves the ink bottle opened and the pen on the blotter which absorbs a round stain. The folded letter touches the bottom of her apron pocket. She closes the bedroom door behind her, picks a piece of lint off the salt sculpture of Our Lady of Luján which adorns the bureau and throws herself face down on the bed. With one hand she squeezes the silk fringe on the edge of the bedspread, the other hand lies still with its palm opened near the boudoir doll that takes up the center of the pillow. She exhales a sigh. She caresses the fringe for several minutes. Suddenly children's voices can be

heard coming up the stairs of the apartment building, she drops the fringe and feels the letter in her
pocket to make sure she hasn't left it in anyone's
reach.

*

Buenos Aires, June 30, 1947

Dear Mrs. Etchepare:

I've just had the joy of getting your letter ahead of time,
but what a disappointment when I read it and realized that
you hadn't gotten the last one I sent. I wrote it over a week
ago, what could have happened? I'm afraid someone might
have taken it out of the box, how do you manage it so that
Celina never goes for the mail? or is it that she doesn't know
you have a mailbox? If Celina finds out I'm after Juan Carlos's letters she might burn them.

Look, Mrs. Etchepare, if it's too much trouble to figure
out which letters were for me, you can send me all of them,
then I'll send back the ones that don't belong to me. He
meant so much to me, Mrs. Etchepare, please forgive the
wrong I may have done, it was all for love.

Please write back soon.

Ever yours,
Nené

She gets up, changes clothes, checks the money in
her purse, goes out, and walks six blocks to the post
office.

*

Buenos Aires, July 14, 1947

Dearest Mrs. Etchepare:

It's been over ten days since I wrote you last and I
haven't gotten any answer. No need to tell you the things that

go through my head! Who knows where that letter is that you didn't get, and then I sent you another one, didn't you get that either? Maybe you changed your mind and don't care for me anymore, did someone tell you something else, another bad thing about me? what did they tell you? If you could only see how poorly I'm getting along, I don't feel like doing anything. I can't talk about it with my husband or the boys, so as soon as I finished giving the boys lunch today, I went to bed so at least I wouldn't have to be putting on an act. I look so worn out lately. I tell the boys that I have a headache, so that they'll leave me in peace for a while. In the morning I go shopping and cook, while the girl does the cleaning, the boys come home from school and we have lunch. My husband doesn't come home for lunch. I keep myself more or less busy in the morning, but the afternoon is so gloomy, Mrs. Etchepare. Luckily the girl washes the dishes for me before she goes home, but today and yesterday, she didn't come, and yesterday I pushed myself to wash the dishes and then went right to bed, but today not even that, I went straight to bed without even cleaning off the table, I couldn't wait to be alone a little. That's the only relief, and I make the room good and dark. Then I can make believe that I'm with you and that we go to poor Juan Carlos's grave and we have a good cry together. It's four o'clock now and it's like spring outside, but instead of going out in the sun for a little I'm shut up indoors so that no one can see me. The dirty dishes are all piled in the kitchen sink, I'll deal with them later on. You know something? a neighbor came in today to return the iron I lent her yesterday and I almost turned my back on her, for no reason. All I need now is for my husband to come home early from the office, I hope to God he's late so that I can send this letter, I'm sure I can. But I'd love to see you and talk over all the things I want to know about these years since I last saw Juan Carlos. I swear to you, Mrs. Etchepare, that when I married Massa, my thing with Juan Carlos seemed over and finished, I continued caring for him as a friend and nothing more. But now I don't know what's wrong with me, I keep thinking that if Celina hadn't spoken badly of me, maybe at this late date Juan Carlos would still be alive and married to some nice girl, or to me.

Here's this clipping from "Our Neighborhood," from the time of the spring festival, I figure it must have been 1936, yes, that's right, because I had just turned twenty. That's where it all began. If it's not too much trouble, please send it back, it's a souvenir, you know.

"GALA CELEBRATION OF THE FIRST DAY OF SPRING

Following a custom established by tradition, the Social Sports Club inaugurated spring with a gala dance which took place on Saturday, September 22, to the pleasant accompaniment of Los Armónicos, a musical band of this locale. At midnight, during an intermission, the charming Nélida Fernández, whose svelte figure adorns these columns, was chosen Miss Spring of 1936. Here her dazzling majesty appears with her predecessor, the alluring María Inés Linuzzi, Miss Spring of 1935. Next, the club's party committee presented a spectacle of yesteryear entitled 'Three Eras of the Waltz,' which was directed by the enthusiastic Mrs. Laura P. Baños, who also read aloud the tasteful commentary. A Viennese waltz from the gay nineties closed this musical cavalcade, executed with remarkable impetuosity by Miss Nélida Fernández and Mr. Juan Carlos Etchepare, who convincingly demonstrated the age-old adage 'Love makes the world go round,' as Mrs. Baños declared. The sensational gowns worn by Misses Rodríguez, Sáenz, and Fernández were in truth particularly outstanding, well matched by the elegance of their companions in their impeccable tails. On the other hand, keep in mind that it is no mean feat to assimilate the historico-musical significance and then express it with ease, after only a few hurried rehearsals, in time borrowed from sleep and rest. A philosophical reflection is fitting here: how many, yes, how many of us wander through this histrionic world reaching each day's end without knowing what role we have played on the great stage of life! If the last couple harvested the thickest applause, this editorial congratulates all with equal fervor. It was a cordial and for many reasons unforgettable evening, heightened by its merit of joyfully uniting a large number of persons who tripped the light fantastic till the wee hours of the morning of the 23rd."

Well, I see that I haven't told you the main thing, the reason why I'm sending you this letter: please write to me soon, because I'm afraid my husband will suspect something if I keep carrying on like a lunatic.

Most affectionately yours,
Nené

Postscript: Don't you want to write me anymore?

She folds the letter and clipping in thirds and puts them in the envelope. She takes them out abruptly, unfolds the letter, and rereads it. She takes the clipping and kisses it several times. She folds the letter and clipping again, puts them in the envelope, which she closes and presses against her breast. She opens a drawer in the kitchen cabinet and hides the envelope among the napkins. She raises a hand to her head and sticks her fingers into her hair, scratches her scalp with short nails polished dark red. She turns on the gas heater to wash the dishes in hot water.

SECOND EPISODE

As long as you can smile,
success can be yours.

(radio commercial for toothpaste,
Buenos Aires, 1947)

Buenos Aires, July 23, 1947

Dearest Mrs. Etchepare:

You haven't written to me for so long! I haven't received a letter of yours for almost four weeks now, nothing's
wrong, I hope. No, I think it's time for our luck to change,
don't you? If something else goes wrong with me I don't
know how I'll have the strength for it. Why is it you don't
write to me?

Today, Saturday, I got my husband to take the kids out
this afternoon, to the game they're playing nearby at the
River Plate Stadium, thank God they left me alone a little because if my husband started picking on me again goodness
knows what I'd answer back. He says I have a sour puss all
the time.

I wonder what you're doing now. Saturday afternoons
in Vallejos someone, the girls, would always come to the
house for a cup of maté. To think that today if I was there on
a visit I still couldn't go to your house for maté, because of
Celina. And why did all that trouble start anyway . . . for
nothing. It all began at the time I started working as a packer
at the Argentine Bargain Store, and because I had been
friends since grammar school with Celina and Mabel who

were already back in Vallejos with their teaching licenses—Mabel a girl with money besides—I began going to the Social Club.

Now Mrs. Etchepare, I admit that that was the wrong move, and all for not listening to mama. And did she hit the nail on the head that time: she told me not to go to the dances at the club. What girls went to the club? Girls who could dress well, or because their parents had a good position, or because they were teachers, but as you'll remember the girls from the stores went to the Recreational Club instead. Mama told me that pushing myself where I didn't belong would only bring trouble. No sooner said than done. That very same year, they were preparing those numbers for the spring festival and they chose me and not Celina. In Mabel's case we knew for sure they'd choose her, because her father cracked the whip at the club. The third girl wasn't a member either, but that was another story entirely, anyway, in the first rehearsal there were the three of us chosen and Mrs. Pagliolo who played the piano, and Mrs. Baños who was teaching us the steps with the special manual she had with all the illustrations marked. The Baños woman ordered us around and wanted Mrs. Pagliolo to play the three waltzes one after the other first so that we could listen to them, when at that point Celina came over and started talking into my ear instead of letting me concentrate on the music. She said she didn't want to be my friend anymore because they had let me into the club thanks to her and now I didn't join her in protest against them leaving her out in the cold. She had already asked me not to accept, in sympathy, but she didn't ask Mabel the same thing, and that made me angry. Why didn't she dare to say the same thing to Mabel? because Mabel had money and I didn't? or because she was a teacher and I hadn't gone further than sixth grade? I don't know why Celina wanted to sacrifice me and not the other one. I had said over and over again to Celina that they weren't leaving her out in the cold, it's just that she was very short and the rented gowns ordered from Buenos Aires all come in medium. The Baños lady was fuming when she saw us talking instead of listening to the music and from that moment on she had it in for me.

My one indignation is this: Celina wanted to hook her brother up with Mabel, and you know that Juan Carlos flirted with her some but that came to an end. Before going steady with me. But just the same Celina seemed to hold on to the hope of having Mabel's family for in-laws.

On weekdays I'd first get out of the store at seven so I was unable to get together with Celina and Mabel, but on Saturdays the two of them would come over to my house at siesta time for maté, and mama would do Mabel's hair for the evening, because she was a girl who couldn't even brush her own hair. The first rehearsal was that Monday, I distinctly remember, and I didn't run into Celina on the street that whole week after, fishy, and on Saturday Mabel came to my house alone. If Mabel didn't come I had already decided to drop the rehearsals. If only she hadn't come, but it was already written that it had to be, in the Book of Destiny. Although it's terrible to think that that afternoon when Mabel's hand knocked on the door and she called to me, it was all written. In that moment I think I dropped what I had in my hand out of pure joy. And now I'm so changed I didn't even do my hair today, I wish I were dead.

But to finish the thing with Celina, I'm going to be frank: what she whispered in my ear was that if it hadn't been for her I wouldn't have set foot in the club, and that everybody knew about Doctor Nastini. Before the Argentine Bargain Store I was Nastini's receptionist and I'd prepare the patients' injections, and when I suddenly left people started saying that there had been something dirty between us, a married man with three children. Well, Mrs. Etchepare, I better stop now because if my husband comes in he'll read the letter, can you just imagine? I'll continue on Monday when he's not around.

Monday, July 25

My Dear Friend:

I'm alone in the world, alone. If I disappear tomorrow my mother-in-law will bring the kids up, or anyone, better than I. Yesterday I locked myself in the room and my husband forced it open, I thought he was going to kill me, but he didn't do anything, he came to the bed and turned me around because I had my head hidden in the pillow, and like a maniac I spit in his face. He said I would pay for that but he kept himself from hitting me. I thought he would break my head open.

This morning to top it off I got it into my head to remember Nastini, and I got upset for nothing, as if the years hadn't passed. I didn't love him like I loved Juan Carlos, the only one I ever loved was Juan Carlos. Nastini took advantage of people. The thing is now I'm never going to be able to see my Juan Carlos again, please don't cremate him! Between Nastini and Celina I lost him, they made him die on me, and now I have to put up with this nuisance Massa for the rest of my life. It was all Celina's fault, that daughter of yours is a viper, beware of her. And while I'm at it I may as well tell you how I came to be marked for life: I was nineteen when they had me go learn nursing with Nastini. One day there was nobody in the office and I had a cough and he began to check me with a stethoscope. Immediately he went too far and began caressing me and I ran into the bathroom red with shame, I put my blouse back on and told him it was my fault, that he should excuse me for wanting to save the money on another doctor. How stupid could I be? It stopped there, but I dreamed of him all night, for fear that he'd corner me again.

One day we had to go by car to a farm for a transfusion, an emergency. It was a woman having hemorrhages after giving birth, and she was saved, after we sweat our heads off. As we were leaving they offered us wine, everyone was happy and I had some. Halfway home Nastini told me to lean against the window and close my eyes to rest the half-hour till we got there. I always did everything he said and when I closed my eyes he kissed me softly. I didn't say anything and he stopped the car. And to think that I'm wasting ink talking about that louse, boy have I paid for one foolish moment!

After that we began seeing each other anywhere we could and in the office itself, just a wall between us and the room where his wife was, she finally realized and I had to go work at the store as a packer. He didn't go after me anymore.

And all for what? Look, I'm going to die with this life I'm leading, nothing but housework and scolding the kids. In the morning, every blessed morning, the fight to get them out of bed, the older one's worse, he's eight years old and in second grade, and luckily the younger one is already going to kindergarten this year, making them drink their milk, dressing them, and taking them to school, spanking them all the way, how tiresome boys are, when it's not one it's the other. On my way back I do the shopping, all at the open market because it's cheaper, but much more tiring because you have to go from stand to stand, and wait on line. Around that time the girl is already in the house cleaning, she washes the clothes too, and I cook and if I give myself time I get rid of the ironing too in the morning, and in the afternoon I can't get the wild Indians to take their nap, how different when they're little babies, how divine, I could eat them up, babies are so adorable, I just have to see a baby on the street or in a

25

photograph and I go crazy, but they grow up so quickly, they get like wild animals. Mine shout all through nap time, at twelve thirty they're already back home, the girl goes to get them. There are some pretty dangerous streets to cross.

How different it was in Vallejos! In the afternoon a girl-friend would come, we would chat, listen to the serial, that is, before I worked at the store, but here, what did I gain from coming to Buenos Aires? I don't know anyone, the neighbors are a bunch of Italians just off the boat, dead from the neck up, and a blonde who must be a kept woman, my husband's positive. I don't know who I can talk to, to nobody, and in the afternoons I try to sew a little and I watch over these animals while they do their homework. Do you know what it's like having two boys stuck in an apartment? they play with their toy cars running races around the furniture. Just as well I don't have good furniture yet, that's why I don't want to invite people from Vallejos to come visit, after they leave they criticize me for not having a fancy house, like it once happened already, I won't tell you who, where does it all get you?

And look it's six o'clock at night now and I already have a splitting headache, like every day, and when my husband comes home it's even worse, he wants dinner right away if it's not ready, and if it's ready, he wants to take a bath first, it's not that he's bad, but as soon as he sets foot in the house I feel like breaking everything, it makes me mad that he comes home, but what fault is it of his if it's his house, and you'll say what did I get married for, but as a newlywed I was never short on patience. I can't stand this life any longer, every day the same old thing.

This morning I went to the zoo again, it's not that far away, ten minutes by bus, because the other day some kid told the children that there was a newborn baby lion, and we went to see him yesterday, Sunday, what a darling! If I have enough money I'm going to buy a puppy or some fancy kind of kitten at the first of the month. What a little darling the lion cub was, how he cuddles against the old lioness, and how they pet each other. This morning it got the best of me and I had to go back to see him alone, nobody was there. The lion cub rolls on the ground with his paws in the air, twists around and then hides under his mother. Like a baby just a few months old. I should go out every day, who was it I told that I was up to my neck in the house and the kids, ah yes, now I remember, the fruit-seller at the market, a nice old woman, one day she said to me that I was always so nervous and I didn't want to wait to be served, then I said what could I do about it, and she answered that you calm down with the years. Does she mean that while I'm young I'll have to put up with whatever it is and then I'm an old woman and everything's lost and that's that? Look, I'm going to tell this guy to go to hell if he's not careful. . . . Do you think I could find a young man who could give me a new life?

I'd like one the way they used to be, nowadays they all look stupid. But not really, I was convinced of that and then the other day I saw such handsome boys, all at once, I hadn't seen a really handsome boy for such a long time and I went to sign the kids up at a club and there were boys there who looked like the ones at the Social Club. Of course they were under twenty-five, and I'm going on thirty. But what jerks they are at that club, you have to be presented by someone else they say, another member, but we hardly know anyone here in Buenos Aires. And I told my husband and he didn't even answer me, as if to say you're on your own. Oh, dearest Mrs. Etchepare, to think that in a while I have to see his face again. If he weren't around, would anyone else notice me? But I'm done with, I've had it, when the Deluge comes, and Judgment Day, I want to go with Juan Carlos, what a consolation the resurrection of the soul and body is for us, Mrs.

Etchepare, that's why I was so worried they'd cremate him. How handsome Juan Carlos was, what a son you had, Mrs. Etchepare, and such a bitch that daughter of yours, if I could get my hands on her this very minute I'd strangle her. She did me in out of envy, yes she did, I don't know what was wrong with her, she let one of the Alvarez boys put his hands on her at sixteen, then she went from one to the other and by the time she was twenty nobody would ask her to dance, for being so clinging, until she got in with the traveling salesmen and then she had no trouble finding someone to take her home after the dance.

But it still made her mad that I could grab her brother, and that's why she told you that Nastini had put his hands on me. But with me there was only one, and because I was a kid, while they dragged her name through the mud till they were bored. And she remained single, that's why she's mad, she remained single! The fool doesn't know that being married is the worst, with a guy who a woman can't get off her back till she's dead. Me, I'd like to be single now, she doesn't know that in the end she won, she's her own master, she's free to go wherever she wants, while I'm condemned to the ball and chain for life!

She violently throws the pen against the sink, takes the written pages, and tears them to bits. A child picks the pen up from the floor, examines it, and tells his mother that it's broken.

*

Buenos Aires, August 12, 1947

Dear Mrs. Etchepare:

I hope these words find you in good health and company. After considerable hesitation I am writing to you, but first of all I must clear something up: I, thank God, have a family that many would like to have, my husband is an irreproachable human being, highly esteemed in his field, he provides for my every need, and my two sons are growing up beautifully, although their mother shouldn't say so, but now that I'm speaking my mind I have to say things the way they are. So that I don't have anything to complain about, but by my letters perhaps you formed a strange idea, just because it got into my head to act weak. I thought how much a mother in your situation must suffer and that's why I thought it would comfort you to know that I accompanied you in the sentiment. I accompanied you, but now you don't want my company anymore, since you don't write me anymore, so here's a piece of information: nobody slams the door on my face and gets away with it.

I don't understand the reason for your silence, but just in case someone has poisoned your ears with lies, I want you to know the whole truth straight from the horse's mouth, then you'll be able to judge me. The only thing I ask of you is that if you've decided not to write me anymore, at least return this letter to me, opened, it's understood, in proof that you read it. Or is that too much to ask?

Well, I shouldn't sound as if it were your fault, the culprit is the one who must have gone to you with stories. And since they want to keep you from seeing the truth, I'm going to have to show it to you. This is my life. . . .

My father couldn't afford for me to study, it would have cost a lot to send me away to study teaching, he was only a gardener, and proud of it, we were. Mama took in ironing and everything she earned went into the savings account for when I got married to have everything I needed for my house. I have it, but not from poor mama's sacrifices, because she lost everything in doctors and medicine when my father passed away. Anyhow, Celina went to school. Then she was worth more than me.

So, it hadn't been long since I started talking to Juan Carlos when he got that cold he couldn't get rid of. Now, this is for Celina's information: the more I kept him talking at the door at night . . . the later he'd get to the DiCarlo widow's house. Everybody said so, that Juan Carlos would go through the gatekeeper's gate at the railroad crossing straight to that possum-playing widow. She was the one who sucked his blood, not I. Until he stopped going, because I didn't want to see him anymore if he continued his relationship with that woman, of course I was acting out of jealousy like any selfish girlfriend, how could I guess the x-rays would show those shadows on the lungs? Now take this down: if Juan Carlos would go to the widow after seeing me it's because with me he behaved like a gentleman.

Then came the trip to Córdoba. He came back looking wonderful, three months later. Now to the heart of the matter: for all that Nastini's wife might have shouted to her husband in front of the maid that he was two-timing her with me, it doesn't prove a thing. But you believed those stories and went against the engagement. And the evidence of my guilt? You never had any.

But did Juan Carlos continue with the widow? no. Listen carefully: I had always smelled a rat, because one day, a little before separating forever, I caught Juan Carlos at a lie. . . . He had a little handkerchief hidden in his coat pocket, tucked in the bottom, a woman's, perfumed, but I wasn't in time to see the initial, embroidered very fancily, but absolutely positive it wasn't E, and the DiCarlo widow's name was Elsa. He told me it belonged to a girl he met in Córdoba, that he was a man and had to live, but when I asked to keep it . . . he snatched it away from me. That means it was a Vallejos girl, don't you think so? I didn't know who to take it out on and I said I was going to cut that stinking widow's head off and he got serious and promised me that the widow

had been shelved, with those words men use that are so offen-
sive to a woman, even though it referred to Elsa DiCarlo.
And I've smelled a rat ever since.

Then came the trouble and we got separated, but it's a
pity that you haven't written to me anymore, because between the two of us maybe we could show up Juan Carlos's
real murderess in her true colors. She's the one your daughter
Celina should be against, and not me. Since Celina is single
and has free time, with no house of her own nor husband or
children to take care of, she could be of some use and help in
the search for truth.

Going back to the subject of Juan Carlos's letters, take
your time and consult your conscience. Then ask yourself if
they don't plainly belong to me.

Sincerely,
Nélida

Postscript: If there's no answer to this letter, this is the last
time I'm writing to you.

Opposite her at the table, one child arduously fills
four lines of his notebook with the word *meow* and
four lines with the word *bowwow*. Among the legs
of the table and chairs another child looks for a
small toy in the shape of a racing car.

THIRD EPISODE

> She fought with the fury of a tigress
> for her man!
> He treated her rough—and she loved it!
>

Picture Album

The covers are in black and white cowhide, the pages of parchment paper. The first page is inscribed in ink: Juan Carlos Etchepare 1934, the second page is blank, and the third is covered with printed old-fashioned lettering interlaced with lances, lariats, spurs, and gaucho belts, forming the words ME AND MY PAMPAS. Next the pages on the right are headed by a printed inscription, the ones on the left are not. Inscriptions: "Here I was born, wild pampas," "Dear old ma and pa," "The bad seed grows," "To school, rain or shine," "First communion: christians yes! barbarians no!" "The young gaucho gets his spurs," "My first gal," "There's never a first without a second," "Serving my flag," "Formal engagement of the gaucho and his gal," "Wedding bells," and "My kids." These last three inscriptions are deliberately covered by large photographs which manage to hide the lettering completely, and following this pattern the rest of the pages on the right are dedicated to large-size photographs, while the ones on the left are filled with groups of small photographs.

First group on the left: an old man and an old woman sitting; bust of an old woman; bust of an old man; street of a village in the Basque provinces of Spain; infant boy; family in a carriage pulled by a white horse. First large photograph on the right: naked, blond infant boy. Second group on the left: a man and a woman—he wears a suit with a vest and a frock coat and she dark long clothes down to her feet; the same couple with two children in their arms; three poses of the woman in the long suit with an old couple and two children. Second large photograph on the right: between an orange tree and a transplanted palm tree there is a well with Spanish ironwork, sitting on the well a three-year-old boy in only white shorts drinks milk from a bottle with a nipple, next to him a woman in a long white dress holds in her arms a naked infant girl who plays with the numerous strands of the woman's necklace. Third group on the left: different poses of the family by the sea in city clothes under a Japanese umbrella. Third large photograph on the right: a garden of small round planters bordered by a small wire fence against which blossoming spikenards and hyacinths lean, a small palm tree in the center of each planter, in the foreground the figure of a little boy in a round-edged jacket, Bohemian-style bow tie, knickers, and white leggings, and the figure of a little girl in a short white dress puffed out by petticoats, above her ringlets a large starched tulle bow.

The following groups on the left, for the rest of the album, belong to different moments of the twenties and thirties, with the frequent presence of an athletic young man invariably smiling and with long light brown hair covering his ears. The remaining pages on the right are filled as already noted by a single large photograph, in the following order: a playground with swings, monkey bars, rings, and bars for gymnastics, in the background a wire fence and behind that some houses spread out on the plains, stunted weeds, and a teenager with light brown hair leaning on a bar looking at the camera, shirt unbuttoned at the neck, mourning tie and arm band, semilong pants to below the knee, long black stockings to the thigh and sandals, next to him another teen-ager with curly black hair that sticks out of his Spanish beret, threadbare clothes, and an expression of wild joy at holding himself up by the exercise ring in midair with one hand only, his legs at a right angle to his torso; the face of a young police officer, oily curly black hair, black eyes, straight nose with strong nostrils, thick mustache, and large mouth, with the dedication "To Juan Carlos, more than a friend a brother, Pancho"; the two young men already described, smiling and sitting at a table covered with beer bottles and four glasses, two young women sitting on their thighs, with low-necks, flabby flesh, faces impaired by too much makeup, and behind the counter of the general store, jugs, a cask of wine, shelves with canned goods, packages of spices, cigarettes, bottles; country scene beneath a carob tree, a tablecloth spread on the grass covered with plates full of breaded veal cutlets, hard-boiled eggs, omelets, and fruit, in the background boys and girls in attitudes of amusement, sitting on the grass next to the tablecloth a girl with short black wavy hair modeled to her perfectly oval face, big black-shadowed eyes, absent expres-sion, small nose, small mouth, bust compressed by a flowered chiffon dress, and a boy with light brown hair, shirt opened where chest hair appears, threatening the plate of veal cutlets with a fork clenched like a dagger; the same girl of the pre-ceding photograph, sitting in a studio pose, with the same in-different expression, her dress draped around the bust, pearl necklace, longer straight hair with a part in the middle and a permanent-wave curl on the ends, the dedication is "A souve-nir from Mabel, June 1936;" a group of three couples posing in period costumes, Restoration, Third Empire, and Gay Nineties respectively, the young woman incarnating the lat-ter era being the closest to the camera, blond hair combed in an upsweep, light eyes with the dazzled expression of someone who sees or imagines something beautiful, nose slightly aquiline, long neck, slim figure; against a background of mountains and poplar trees, wearing a poncho, his pullover inside the wide white pants with a high belt up to his diaphragm, the young man with light brown hair, thinner but suntanned and wearing his characteristic smile, the dedication "With love as always for my old lady and little sister, Juan Carlos, Cosquín 1937"; toasting cider beside a birthday cake a short young woman, despite the high pompadour set on her forehead, with a square neckline and a brooch at each corner, an older woman somberly dressed, and the young man with light brown hair, thinner, his eyes notably larger and hollowed into his face, looks at his drink with a barely sketched smile; the young man with light brown hair in a chaise against a background of mountains and cactus, the details of which are blurred since the photograph has been taken almost against the light.

Young Lady's Bedroom, 1937

Entering on the right one sees a three-quarter bed, with the headboard against the wall, and above a crucifix consisting of a wooden cross and a bronze Christ. At the left of the bed a small library of four shelves full of college textbooks and some novels, the former covered in brown paper and labeled "María Mabel Sáenz—Our Lady of the Pillar College— Buenos Aires." To the right of the bed the night table and lamp with a white gauze green-specked shade, the same as the window curtains and bedspread. Under the glass on the table a postcard from Pearl Beach in Mar del Plata, a postcard from Inca's Bridge in Mendoza, and the photograph of a stout young man in impeccable country wear next to a horse and a ranch hand who adjusts the cinch. At the foot of the bed a rabbit skin in white, black, and brown. On the wall opposite

35

the bed a window, on one side of it a mantelpiece laden with dolls, all with natural hair and movable eyes, and on the other side a bureau with a mirror. On the bureau a hand mirror and brush set with velvet handles, placed in a circle around a calf-skin picture frame with the photograph of a girl seated, her dress draped around the bust, pearl necklace, straight hair with a part in the middle and a permanent wave on the ends. Other decorations on the wall: mother-of-pearl baptismal font, a group of three school pennants, Saint Teresita carved in wood, and a group of four framed photographs taken at different moments during a country cookout marked by the presence of a stout young man in impeccable country wear. The remaining wall opposite the entrance door, entirely covered by a wardrobe; in the center of the ceiling a chandelier. Bed, night table, bureau, mirror, wardrobe, and chandelier in the style called colonial, in dark wood and prominent iron hardware; the mantelpiece and bookshelves, as contrast, in smooth light varnished wood. Dresses, coats, and two white-starched box-pleated aprons are hanging in the wardrobe. Tied to the bar holding the hangers there's a small silk sachet full of fragrant dry lavender. In the same wardrobe one side contains drawers full of underwear, blouses, handkerchiefs, stockings, towels, and sheets. Hidden among embroidered linen sheets is the flowered wool lace-edged cover of a hot water bottle. Inside the cover two scientific books entitled *Education for the Married Couple* and *The Truth About Love*. Between said books a photograph where with other young people one can see a couple seated beside a picnic ta-blecloth, she with an absent air and he pointing to a plate with a fork. Behind the photograph one can read the following text: "My love: this was the hapiest day of my life. I never dreemed that I could make you mine! The first day of spring. Hide this picture till every thing gets straightened out. I'm writing this wreckless stuff on purpose so that you can't show it to any body, because in that pose I look like a gerk and a bit 'high.' You know they're trying to make me look like a lush around here.

"This very moment I'd grab you by the hand and carry you up to the sky, or at least to some place far from here. Remember the weping wilows next to the little lake? I'll never forget them.

"I love you more and more, Juan Carlos, September 21, 1935."

In the same drawer, under the white paper attached to the bottom with tacks, two issues of the magazine *Feminine World* are hidden, dated April 30 and June 22, 1936. In the Lonelyhearts column there are letters of consultation from a reader who signs "Bewildered Soul" and the respective answers given by María Luisa Díaz Pardo, editor of the column. The text in the first issue is as follows:

"Dear Friend:
    I've been buying this magazine for almost a year now and I always read your fascinating section. But I never imagined that one day I'd have to resort to your advice. I'm eighteen years old, I'm a teacher, just graduated, and my parents are comfortably situated. A nice boy, but of uncertain future, loves me. He is still very young and can change, but my family doesn't like him. He works as a bookkeeper but has had arguments with his superiors for frequent absenteeisms. He has gone through a period of continual colds and often feels tired. I believe him but the rumor in circulation is that he's too interested in having a good time, he plays the field, and at least once a week gets drunk with his chums. He's been taking me out on excursions and to dances for some months, at first I was sure I loved him with all my heart but each day (he comes to the street door in the evening after work, I wait for him there so he doesn't have to come in or ring the bell, and we roam around the streets or in the square a little and if it's very cold we take shelter in the entranceway, our intimacy not going any further than that),

but each day as I said, when he leaves and I go into the house I have to put up with my parents' rebukes, rebukes which like each drop of water wear away the stone. So that each day I await his arrival with pleasure but as soon as I see his seemly figure approaching I'm already nervously thinking that my mother might come out, or even worse, my father, and demand of my admirer some explanation or make some cutting insinuation, all of which often makes me irritable with him. I tell him that it's the natural nervousness from my first year working as a teacher, of nothing less than fifth graders. But what is making me irritable is the doubt: do I love him or don't I love him? Lately a new opposing element has come into the picture: a young rancher of English origin, less seemly than "him" but of a pleasant personality, has used his friendship with father to make his way into the house and pay me compliments. And here's the dilemma: he has invited me and a companion (I shall choose my mother's sister) to spend the four-day holiday coming up on May 25 at his ranch, and my parents insist that I go, and "he" is firmly opposed. I have decided . . . to go, because in that way I shall know if I miss "him" or not. But what if he keeps his word and doesn't look my way anymore as he has in effect forewarned?

Friend, I await your valuable advice. Yours,
Bewildered Soul (Province of Buenos Aires)."

The editor's answer is as follows:

"Enviable Bewildered Soul:
I don't envy the bewilderment of your soul but rather all that you have in life. I don't think that you love your admirer enough to confront a break with your parents. Your case is typical of young girls brought up in the heart of a happy and prosperous family. To continue your flirtation (excuse the term) would mean destroying that family harmony you already feel threatened. And believe me, for a flirtation one shouldn't pay such a price. You are very young and can wait for the knight on the white horse who is to everyone's taste. Have a good time at the ranch, study English, and in case

38

you two have to make signs in order to communicate please don't nod your head yes too often! By using that sign sparingly you will conquer the world and, even more important, you will secure your happiness and that of your parents. As always at your service,

María Luisa Díaz Pardo."

The letter of consultation in the June 22, 1936 issue is as follows:

"Dear Friend:

Life has played me a mean trick. Your advice to me was correct, but unseen complications have arisen. In effect my admirer was angry at my going to that ranch, and the incident served to cut off our relationship. I must confess that my stay at the ranch was not what I had hoped for since that gentleman and I spent long moments face to face without uttering a word. When it came time to say good-by he tried to get a promise out of me but I told him that that didn't seem right to me, since I had inspired neither words nor gestures in him. His answer was that the English are like that, people of few words, that he envied the blabbering Latins, but that even in silence he felt comfortable with me. As far as gestures were concerned, which was my way of saying that he didn't pick flowers for me, or that he didn't select records which I liked (he always made us listen to his favorites), he understood me wrong, he thought I was reproaching him for not making advances to me. With regard to that he clarified that if our lives were to join, there would be time for that. How unromantic, don't you think so? I sincerely was waiting for a passionate kiss to find out if he pleased me or not. In any case I didn't promise him anything, what does it mean to nod your head yes? I don't know how to make that sign! and as you anticipated, that has had its effect because he has written to my parents inviting us all for the winter vacations, two whole weeks. We might accept. But what I have to tell you now is so sad that it overwhelms me with grief and I'm not sure how to express myself.

A few days after coming back from the country my father called me aside, our family doctor was awaiting us in his study. In the strictest confidence he told me that my ex-admirer had somewhat weak lungs, according to recent analysis he suffers from the beginnings of a certain highly contagious illness. I couldn't believe my ears and even thought it was a trick of father's. The doctor added that I should avoid his company and that given the misunderstanding we had scarcely two weeks ago I should take advantage of that excuse and not see him again, until he was cured. The next day I happened to see my ex-admirer's mother and sister in a store and I noticed that they were affectionate with me but looked terribly sad. I was convinced that all was, unfortunately, true. Besides, the next day, without consulting me, my mother told me that at five we had an appointment with the doctor to take some x-rays of me. We've already seen the results: I'm healthy.

Now then, what can I do to help my dear friend? In this moment I am ashamed for having made him suffer. Perhaps one day life will bring us together again, because I believe I really love him, or is it only pity? I beg of you, friend and adviser, help me to elucidate my true feelings. Anxiously I remain,

Bewildered Soul (Province of Buenos Aires)"

The editor's reply is as follows:

"Bewildered but Generous Soul:
I am confident that you will forge ahead. Surely what you feel for him now is pity, added to the nostalgia of more joyous days. I've consulted a doctor and he has told me that you can see him as a friend, taking precautions. Try not to get too close and get used to patting him on the back when you meet him, while when saying good-by you can give him your hand, since you will immediately have the chance to wash your hands in soap and water and then soak them in alcohol. Yes, offer him your friendship, but not in a sudden or suspicious manner, wait for an opportune moment, since those affected by that illness become very susceptible. Don't let him see your pity. Given his character, that would hurt him most.

As far as your future is concerned, don't forget that making signs can be a strange but beautiful language. As ever,

María Luisa Díaz Pardo"

In this same issue of the magazine *Feminine World*, the pictures on two of the pages have been cut out, with scissors, corresponding to the following captions: "Slick cocktail gown in moiré silk, with Juliet headpiece, the latest fashion inspired by the fabulous Metro-Goldwyn-Mayer production *Romeo and Juliet*, by the immortal W. Shakespeare. M-G-M Photo." and "The new movie industry sensation, Deanna Durbin, suggests this dazzling cycling attire for the young girl, in white linen, its edges brightened by lively red rick-rack. Universal Pictures Photo."

Behind the window of the room already described a first courtyard can be seen, covered by grapevines which climb and curl around a wire ceiling, beyond that planters with rose and jasmine bushes, lastly a large fig tree, taller than the brick wall blocking off the neighboring lot where they are erecting the two-story building destined to be the new police station. One of the bricklayers at the construction site protects himself from the sun with a Spanish beret from which his curly hair sticks out, black like the thick mustache over his large mouth and like the eyes which look from the scaffolds, through the branches of the fig tree, in the direction of the courtyard of rose and jasmine bushes, grapevines, and windows adorned by white gauze green-specked curtains.

Memo Book 1935

MARCH—TUESDAY 14, SAINT MATILDE, QUEEN. Hairy old memo book! I'm starting you off with a widow, who's already on the hook.

WEDNESDAY 15, SAINT CAESAR, MARTYR. Asked fifteen pesos advance for gift for widow's neighbor, widow's gift, and general expences.

SATURDAY 18, SAINT GABRIEL, ARCHANGEL. Crap game at the Gaucho Inn, Perico comes with car.

SUNDAY 19, SAINT JOSEPH. Shindig at the club. Paid two rounds for Pepe and Barros bruthers. They owe me for next time.

WEDNESDAY 22, SAINT LEA, NUN. Date at 7 P.M. Clarita.

THURSDAY 23, SAINT VICTORIANO, MARTYR. Date at the Gaucho Inn, Amalia, produce car.

SATURDAY 25, THE ANNUNCIATION OF THE BLESSED VIRGIN MARY. Widow, 2 A.M.

SUNDAY 26, PASSION SUNDAY. Promise go to Mass with mama and Celina, 10 A.M. (in a stretcher?)

THURSDAY 30, AMADEUS, HOLY MAN. Date at the Gaucho Inn, Amalia, ask Perico for car. Cancel, flu, ask Pancho tell Amalia. No, Pancho dangerous, let fatso wait, sitting so she won't get tired.

APRIL—TUESDAY 4, SAINT ISIDORE, MARTYR. Got paid minus advance, s.o.b.!

THURSDAY 6, SAINT CELESTINE, MARTYR. Missed work, flu, couff, bed, relapse.

FRIDAY 7, SAINT ALBERT, MARTYR. Missed work, flu, bed.

MONDAY 10, SAINT TERENCE, BISHOP. Missed work, flu, up around the house.

TUESDAY 11, SAINT LEO I, THE GREAT POPE. Back to the yoke.

THURSDAY 20, SAINT ADALGISA, VIRGIN. Won 120 pesos crap game at club!

SATURDAY 22, SAINT ANSELM, BISHOP. Take Pancho crap game the Gaucho Inn, the Barros have it in for me.

SUNDAY 23, SAINT ALBERT, MARTYR. Wait Clarita after Mass, apoligize. Scratch Clarita, she can shove it. Swear word of honor faithful to widow, alias the easy-going.

THURSDAY 27, SAINTS IDA AND ZITA. Missed date widow, fault red wine the Gaucho Inn, Pancho ass pucked on table. Remember apoligize widow, alias the good piece.

JULY—FRIDAY 7, SAINT RITA. Train from B.A. arrive 8:15 P.M., girls home from school. Take a look.

SATURDAY 8, SAINT ADRIAN, MARTYR. Shindig Social Club. Lend dough Pancho crap game. Lost. Scored at the Social Club.

SUNDAY 9, SAINT PROCOPIUS, MARTYR. Missed date Mass, unpardonable. The prettiest chick in the world left in the lerch by a poor retch. Whole day stuck in the house, excuse couff. The truth of the pudding: it's great to sleep till twelve!

MONDAY 10, SAINT FELIX, MARTYR. I saw her! she believed sister's story, thanks Celina! "One can see you mean well, you prefer to stay home Sunday so you can get rid of your couff and work Monday." One can see you're a doll . . .

THURSDAY 13, SAINT ANACLETUS, POPE. Haven't seen her for three days. Date widow 11:30 P.M.

FRIDAY 14, SAINT BONAVENTURE. Thanks Saint Bonaventure! Met her coming out of novena. Mabel, Mabel, Mabel, Mabel. At 10 P.M. movie date with Celina and little brother (at your service). The movie I least understood in my whole life.

SATURDAY 15, SAINT HENRY, EMPEROR. Intimate shindig Mabel's house, good-night at entranceway. The world is mine.

SUNDAY 16, OUR BLESSED LADY OF CARMEL. She left me for Buenos Aires. I can become a num and get into the school. Who's to prevent me? It's my vocasion.

· ·

SEPTEMBER—TUESDAY 10, SAINT CASIMIR, MARTYR. Ten days to go.

WEDNESDAY 11, SAINT HERMAN, KING. Nine days to go.

THURSDAY 12, SAINT SERAPHIM, BISHOP. Eight days to go.

FRIDAY 13, SAINT EDWARD, KING. Seven days to go.

SATURDAY 14, SAINT CALLISTUS, BISHOP. Six days to go. They skinned 97 pesos off me at Gaucho.

SUNDAY 15, SAINT TERESA, VIRGIN. Keep promiss, go to Mass. Five days to go.

Monday 16, Saint Gallo, Martyr. Four days to go. Date Amalia in Gaucho, get car Perico.

Tuesday 17, Saint Hedwig, Martyr. Three days to go.

Wednesday 18, Saint Luke, Evangelist. Day after tomorrow . . .

Thursday 19, Saint Peter of Alcantara. Tomorrow!

Friday 20, Saint Irene, Virgin. Train from Buenos Aires arrives 8:15. She's prettier than I remembered!!! We shook hands. In front of her old lady.

Saturday 21, Saint Matthew, Apostle. First day of Spring, student's holiday, how you take your time in coming! Picnic excursion on La Carola Ranch. Date 7:30 A.M. in front the Modern House coffee shop. Celina brings food . . . I AM THE HAPIEST BEING ON EARTH AND PROMISE BEFORE GOD TO BEHAVE LIKE A MAN, I SWEAR NOT TO TELL ANY BODY AND TO MARRY HER.

Sunday 22, Saint Maurice, Martyr. Train leaves 10:30 A.M. How faraway December is. . . . She threw me a kiss with her hand in front of her old lady. By now she must be at school.

FOURTH EPISODE

My obsession, heartbreak tango,
plunged my soul to deepest sin,
as the music of that tango
set my poor heart all a-spin.

(from Roldan's "Blame That Tango")

Thursday, April 23, 1937, the sun rose at 5:50 A.M. Light winds blew from north to south, it was partly cloudy, with the temperature at 57 degrees Fahrenheit. Nélida Enriqueta Fernández slept till 7:45 A.M., at which time her mother woke her up. Nélida's hair was divided into locks tied with strips of paper, kept in place by a thin black net which covered her whole skull. A black slip took the place of a nightgown. She put on a pair of old backless espadrilles. It took her thirty-seven minutes to prepare her daily hairdo and put on makeup, interrupted by five sips of the cup of maté which her mother brought to her. While she brushed her hair she thought of the argument she had had the day before with the cashier, of the disadvantage of having coffee with milk and bread and butter for breakfast, of the faint feeling in the stomach she would experience at 11:00 A.M., of the advantage of having a pack of mints in her pocket, of her always brisk and rapid walk home at noon, of the routine struggles with Juan Carlos the night before at the door of her house, and of the need to remove the mud from her white shoes with the appropriate liquid. Putting on her makeup she thought of the seductive possibilities of her face and of the different opinions heard on the positive or negative effect of the natural shadow of rings under the eyes. At 8:30 she left her house. She wore a blue cotton uniform buttoned down the front, with round collar and long sleeves. At 8:42 she entered the Argentine Bargain Store. At 8:45 she was at her post behind the wrapping table, beside the cashier and her cash register. The other employees, twenty-seven in all, were also putting their work posts in order. At 9:00 the doors opened to the public. The packer did her first package at 9:15, a dozen and a half buttons for a man's suit. Between 11:00 and 12:00 she had to hurry so as not to keep the customers waiting. The doors closed at 12:00, the last customer left at 12:07. At 12:21 Nélida entered her house, washed her hands, noticed that her father—sharpening pruning shears in the shed out back—had seen her come in and had bent his head without greeting her. She sat at the table, with her back to the wood-burning stove. Her father came in to wash his hands in the sink filled with a dirty pot and scolded her for saying good-night to Juan Carlos, the night before, at almost midnight, talking at the gate from 10:00 on despite the cold wind. Nélida drank her soup without answering, her mother served boiled potatoes and salted liver. Each drank three-quarters of a glass of wine. Nélida said that the cashier had not greeted her when she entered the store. She cut a few grapes off a bunch, and went to lie down in her room. She thought of the store manager, of the removable starched collar he always wore, of the saleswoman known to be his mistress, of the advantage of finding them in the basement in a compromising position to thus assure them of her total discretion and in turn merit a favor, of Doctor Nastini and his becoming short-sleeved doctor's shirt with the belt in the back, of how he didn't look as good when he took off his shirt, of Mrs. Nastini's imported Chinese silk dressing gown, of the maidservant Big Fanny's gray uniform, of the front of

Doctor Nastini's house with the black marble base over a yard high contrasting with the white plaster of the rest of the wall, of the brick front of Juan Carlos's house and the courtyard with palm trees that could be seen from the street, of the starched collar on Juan Carlos's striped shirt, of his complaining that the starch irritated the skin of his neck, of his request that she kiss the affected skin, of the struggles that followed, of the possibility that Juan Carlos would drop her if he found out there had been another man in her life, of the possibility of not letting Juan Carlos know until a few weeks before the marriage, of the possibility that Juan Carlos would find out on the wedding night, of the possibility that Juan Carlos would strangle her in a Buenos Aires hotel on the wedding night, of the smell of disinfectant in Doctor Nastini's office, of Doctor Nastini's olive-green car, of the sick woman whose life they had saved in a farmhouse, of the sunlight that came through the window and kept her from falling asleep, of the effort of getting up and closing the Venetian blinds, of the darkened room and the relief it meant for her eyes. At 1:30 P.M. her mother woke her up with a cup of sweet maté, at 2:00 she had already dressed and put on fresh makeup, at 2:13 she entered the store, invigorated by the brisk walk. At 2:15 she stationed herself punctually behind her wrapping table. She was surprised to discover how little medium-sized paper was left in the roll, looked around for the manager, did not see him, thought of the possibility of the manager passing by and not seeing her at her post while she was down in the basement getting the necessary refill. The cashier was not seated at her stool yet, Nélida ran down to the basement and did not find the refill. On her way back she came face to face with the manager who immediately put his hand on his waist and took the watch out of his pocket with a severe gesture. He said to Nélida that she was late to her post. Nélida replied that she had gone to look for something

47

in the basement and had not found it, once at her post she showed him the little paper left in the roll. The manager replied that there was enough for the day and that if she finished it she could use the big roll and calculate the width of the roll as the length of the package. Without looking at Nélida he added that she had to use her ingenuity and no matter what be at her post on time. He said this as he was walking away, to avoid an answer. At 2:30 the doors opened. It turned out to be easy to wrap things from the Notions section and hard to do the hats. Usually what Nélida liked to wrap most was the special offer of a dozen jingling buttons sewn to a square piece of cardboard; on the other hand she detested the potted plants from the new Evergreen Nursery section. She exchanged cordial words with the customer who appreciated the care she took in not breaking the feather on her hat during the process of wrapping it. The cashier joined in on the conversation with flattering comments, and when the customer left the cashier looked at Nélida for the first time that day and told her that the manager was a louse. At 6:55 they began closing the doors and at 7:10 the last customer left with a package containing a zipper and the corresponding receipt. Before leaving Nélida told the manager in an impersonal manner that there were no more refills for medium-sized paper in the basement and walked out without waiting for an answer. The air outside was pleasant and she thought that it wouldn't be cold later on by the door to her house. Passing the League bar she looked inside with apparent indifference. She saw Juan Carlos's disheveled hair from the back, at a table of four where a game of dice was going on. She stopped for a moment hoping Juan Carlos would turn his head. She could not resist the impulse to look toward the other tables. Doctor Nastini was having an apéritif with a friend and looking at her. Nélida blushed and resumed walking. Her mother was drying the bathroom floor and told her there was little hot water left because her father had just bathed. Nélida asked sullenly if she had washed the bathtub well. Her mother in turn asked if she considered her a dirty fishwife and reminded her that there was always a clean bathtub awaiting her when she came home from the store. Nélida touched with disgust the piece of laundry soap that she'd have to use for her bath. She sank into the half-full bathtub. With only her head out of the water she thought of a new product from the Quality Gifts section: an oval cellophane box full of translucent green tablets for perfuming bath water. She was suddenly alarmed at the possibility that the cheap soap would leave a smell of disinfectant on her skin; the water from the faucet was already coming out cold when she finished carefully rinsing herself. Once dry she smelled her hands and felt relieved, she thought of the fact that Juan Carlos didn't want to go dancing at the Social Club on Sunday afternoons anymore, preferring to take her to the movies, she thought of the fact that she didn't have any other girlfriend at the club, she thought of Celina, of her green eyes, she thought of cats with green eyes, she thought of the possibility of being friends with a cat, friends with a she-cat, rubbing its back, she thought of an old she-cat with scabs, how to cure its scabs, take it something to eat, pick the prettiest dish from the cupboard and fill it with fresh milk for an old scabby she-cat, she thought of the fact that Juan Carlos's mother on her way home from the novena service greeted them unenthusiastically on Sunday after the movie, she thought of a natural or accidental death for Nastini's wife, of the possibility of Nastini asking her to be his second wife, of the possibility of marrying Nastini and abandoning him before the honeymoon, of the rendezvous she would plan with Juan Carlos at a refuge among the snows of a winter resort. Nastini on the train in a silk robe, he comes out of the lavatory and goes down the aisle to the stateroom, knocks gently on the door, waits in vain for an answer, opens the door, and finds a letter saying that she got off at the preceding station, that he shouldn't look for her, meanwhile Juan Carlos keeps the rendezvous and reaches the refuge, finds her in black pants and black high-neck sweater, bobbed platinum blond hair, they embrace, Nélida finally surrenders to her true love. Nélida thought of the possibility of not drying the bathroom floor. After dressing she dried it. Her mother ate the leftovers of the salted liver and Nélida a veal cutlet with a lettuce and egg salad. Her father didn't sit at the table as he usually did at night. At 8:30 they tuned in the radio to a station that played a program of Spanish songs. While listening her mother cleared the table, Nélida wiped the oilcloth with a damp rag and set down her sewing box and a dress which was ready except for the buttonholes. At 9:00 the Spanish program ended and a recital of Gaucho poetry began. At 9:20 Nélida began to redo her hair and makeup. At 9:48 she stood at the entrance of the house by the gate. At 10:05 she could see Juan Carlos a block away. At 10:20 Nélida and Juan Carlos saw that her parents' bedroom light was already out. They left the sidewalk and moved toward the house. As usual Nélida leaned her back against the metallic column that supported the tin awning. As usual she closed her eyes and received on her lips the first kiss of the night. Without realizing she decided that if the old beggar woman at the church door put a dagger in her hand she'd gladly kill Celina. Juan Carlos kissed her again, this time holding her very close in his arms. Nélida received caresses, more kisses, a compliment, and embraces of varied intensity. With her eyes closed she asked Juan Carlos if he was taking advantage of his leave of absence to rest up and also asked him what he had done that afternoon before going to the bar. He didn't answer her. Nélida opened her eyes when she realized that he had let go of her and was taking a step toward the hedge, carefully trimmed by her father. Nélida opened her eyes even more when she saw Juan Carlos reach out and pull off a branch, then she argued that she told him everything she did and didn't see why he couldn't do the same. Juan Carlos replied that men needed to keep certain things to themselves. Nélida observed his abundant locks of hair, some of them metallized by the white light of the bulb on the municipal lamppost standing in the middle of the street, and without knowing why, she thought of public lots covered with bushes and long bending grass, lit at night by the light bulbs of municipal lampposts; Nélida looked at his eyes, not green like Celina's but light brown and without knowing why she thought of luscious honey jars; Juan Carlos closed his eyes as she caressed his uncombed hair and upon seeing his thick curved lashes, Nélida, without knowing why, thought of spreading eagle wings; Nélida looked at his straight nose, thin mustache, thick lips, asked him to show her his teeth and without knowing why she thought of old-time mansions with white balustrades and tall shaded colonnades that she'd seen in textbooks; Nélida looked at his Adam's apple located between the two strong muscles of his neck, and his broad shoulders, and without knowing why she thought of the knotty rugged trees of the wild pampas: the ombu and the oak were her favorite trees. At 11:20 Nélida let him put his hand under her blouse. At 11:30 Juan Carlos said good-night objecting to her selfishness. At 11:47 Nélida finished dividing her hair into many sections fastened with paper. Before going to sleep she thought of the fact that Juan Carlos's face had no flaws.

The aforementioned Thursday April 23, 1937, Juan Carlos Jacinto Eusebio Etchepare woke up at 9:30 when his mother knocked on the door and went into the room. Juan Carlos did not respond to his mother's words of affection. The cup of tea remained on the night table. Juan Carlos wrapped himself in a bathrobe and went to brush his teeth. The bad taste in his mouth disappeared. He went back to his room, the tea was lukewarm, he called his mother and asked her to reheat it. At 9:55 he drank an almost boiling cup of tea in bed, with the conviction that the heat would do his chest good. He thought of the possibility of constantly drinking very hot things and wrapping himself in hot cloths, with his feet beside a hot water bottle, his head wrapped in a woolen scarf with only his nose and mouth uncovered to finally rid his respiratory organs of their imperfection. He thought of the possibility of putting up with days and weeks of stifling in bed, until the dry heat eliminated the dampness in his lungs; dampness and cold made moss grow on his lungs. He went back to sleep, he dreamed of reddish bricks, the pit where they mix the materials for bricks, the pit of burning lime, the soft raw bricks, the baking bricks, the hardened indestructible bricks, the bricks outdoors at the construction site of the new police station, Pancho was showing him a pile of unusable broken bricks which are returned to the oven to be crushed and baked again, Pancho then explained to him that at a construction site nothing is wasted. His mother woke him at 12:00, Juan Carlos was sweating. As he got up he felt very weak. He asked his mother if there was hot water for a bath and if his beard was too dark to go to his doctor's appointment without shaving. His mother answered that he should shave right then, and that he should do it every day when he got up. She added that the night before he had gone to bed very late, and that the girls would fall for a boy like him just the same even though he didn't shave moments before seeing them. She added that when he returned to his job at the mayor's office he'd have to get used to getting out of bed ahead of time to shave, because it was on his job that he had to look his best and not on dates. At that moment Celina arrived in her white teacher's smock with several books under her arm, her mother exchanged looks with her and asked Juan Carlos where he had been the night before till 3:00 in the morning and if he had lost money playing cards. Juan Carlos answered that he hadn't been gambling. His mother said that then he had been with Nélida. Juan Carlos assented. His mother asked how was it possible that her parents let her converse on the sidewalk until 3:00 in the morning, and on not getting an answer she told Juan Carlos that if he wanted to wash up and shave before lunch he should please do so immediately. At 12:55 Juan Carlos came out of the bathroom showered, but unshaven. Entering the dining room he began to notice the symptoms of his usual hot flushes. His mother and Celina were sitting at the table. Juan Carlos held on to the back of his chair, thought of going back to his bedroom and getting into bed, both women looked at him, Juan Carlos sat down. Noodle soup, then grilled steak, and mashed potatoes. Juan Carlos's steak was thick and juicy, cooked rare, to his taste. As he began to cut it he felt his forehead bathed in sweat. His mother told him to go to bed, it was dangerous to perspire and then get chilled. Juan Carlos didn't answer and went to his room. A few minutes later they took the meal to his bed on a tray. Juan Carlos found that the steak was cold. They took it back to the grill, Celina let it touch the iron on one side and then the other just a few seconds so that it wouldn't cook too much. His mother and Celina were standing in the room looking at him, waiting for some order. Juan Carlos asked them to go finish their lunch. Listlessly he finished his plate. When his mother came in with dessert, a baked apple, Juan Carlos was feeling better already and said that before the rash of colds and bronchitis he had sometimes felt very hot after a shower, and that he as well as the rest of the family were senselessly influencing each other by suggestion. Lunch agreed with him. His mother and Celina would take a siesta, he went out in the same clothes he wore at lunch—

gray flannel pants, light blue flannel checkered shirt, long-sleeved blue pullover—plus a dark brown leather jacket with a zipper. That garment, characteristic of rich ranchers, caused a variety of reactions on the street. Juan Carlos smiled in satisfaction at the scornful look of the bakery owner who was talking to a caterer on the sidewalk. The sun warmed the air but in the shade it was cold. Juan Carlos chose the sunny side and opened the zipper of his jacket. At 2:48 he reached the League, the most fashionable bar in town. At a table a gray-haired man drinking coffee waved to him enthusiastically. Juan Carlos agreed to accompany him to a cattle yard a few miles from town, but first he ordered a cup of coffee and made a telephone call: talking so that no one would hear him he gave the nurse a false excuse so that he could cancel the appointment. Juan Carlos thought of the possibility that the doctor, after checking him over, would tell him that the week of rest had done him good; of the possibility that he would make him prolong the rest period beyond the following week, the end of his leave; of the possibility that he would make him rest the whole winter, as he had already insinuated; of the possibility that he had discovered a tremendous mix-up in the x-rays: that plate with a faint shadow in the right lung was not his but someone else's, some poor fool condemned to die after two or three years of depriving himself of women and other fun. At 3:50 Juan Carlos was strolling in the sun on a plot near the corral where his friend was talking to some ranch hands. The land was light and dark brown, around an Australian water tank grew dwarf camomile plants with green stems and yellow and white flowers. Juan Carlos remembered that as a child they had always told him not to chew the wild camomile flower, because it was poisonous. At 4:15 the sun's light was weaker and Juan Carlos thought that, had he gone to the doctor's office, by then he would already know the state of his health. At 4:30 his friend stopped the car opposite the construction site of the new police station so that Juan Carlos could get out. They separated till later at the bar. Juan Carlos entered the site and asked an electrician where Pancho was. In the future courtyard of the police station three workers were plastering the walls of the toilet and showers for low-ranking personnel. Pancho shouted to him that he had fifteen minutes to go, Juan Carlos shrugged his shoulders, Pancho gave him the "up yours" sign and continued working but a few seconds later ran over to him with the feeling of doing something naughty and handed his friend the toy he coveted most, to keep him busy. Juan Carlos smoked his friend's cigarette on the sidewalk, conscious of each puff. A nearly adolescent girl walked by and looked at him. At 4:55 the two friends went into the only place where Pancho would dare to go in overalls, a tavern opposite the railroad station. Juan Carlos asked him if in order to keep alive he would give up women, drinking, and smoking. Pancho told him not to bring that subject up again and to drink down his grappa. Juan Carlos said he really meant it. Pancho didn't answer. Juan Carlos was going to say something else but didn't: if he had to give up living like healthy people he'd rather die, but that even if they didn't take his women and cigarettes away he'd rather die if it was in exchange for working like a dog the whole day long for three pennies and then going home to a shack to wash up under the cold water of a pump. Pancho asked him if he had noticed how the courtyard at the site looked, in daylight. Juan Carlos asked Pancho if he too had had sexual intercourse the night before. Pancho said that being the end of the month he didn't have money to go to the Gaucho Inn. Juan Carlos promised to go with him on the 1st and meantime advised him to make a play for Big Fanny, Doctor Nastini's housemaid. Pancho asked him why they called her Big Fanny and Juan Carlos answered that her rear end stuck out like the tail of a hen, in her aunt's shack where she had been brought up they'd always called her that. At 5:40 they closed the discussion on Big Fanny with Juan Carlos's advice to Pancho that if he didn't hurry and grab her someone else would get there first. At 6:00 he entered the League alone, he noticed that no one was coughing. Peretti the farm agent, Juárez the storekeeper, and Rolla the veterinarian were at the table by the window: a cuckold, an idiot, and a tightwad respectively, thought Juan Carlos. At a nearby table were three bank clerks: three starving corpses, thought Juan Carlos. At another table, Doctor Nastini and the jeweler-watchmaker Roig: a son of a bitch with foul breath and a bootlicking weasel, thought Juan Carlos. He went toward a table in the back where they waited for him to play poker, three landholders were seated around him: one more cuckold, another cuckold, and a lucky lush, thought Juan Carlos. He was very hot but after taking off his jacket the feeling passed; he contemplated the possibility of winning like the day before, to cover all his bar and movie expenses of the two weeks of leave, and concentrated on the game. An hour later he felt an itching in his throat, repressed the cough, and looked around for the waiter: the second cup of coffee was not coming. His feet were cold, but from the waist up he radiated hot vapor, he unbuttoned his collar. The waiter brought the coffee. The itch in his throat increased. Juan Carlos quickly removed the paper from the sugar cubes and without waiting for them to dissolve drank down the whole cup. He touched his forehead as if casually, hot but still dry, he thought that the cold entrance gate at Nené's house was to be blamed for it all. Just then he remembered that she must have passed by on the sidewalk already. At 8:15 having lost only a few cents he went home and directly to the bathroom. He shaved with special soap, a brush, and a pitcher of boiling water that his mother brought to him. At 8:40 they sat down at the table. Celina talked about Mabel's mother being desperate because with the maid's absence she had no time to rest, and right at cattle auction time, with Mabel's fiancé in Vallejos, a constant visitor at the house. Dinner ended, Celina played a song on the piano from the new music book just arrived from Buenos Aires entitled *Great Melodies by Mexican Serenaders*. Juan Carlos reminded them that it was time for the daily cigarette his doctor permitted him. Trying not to give too much importance to the subject his mother then asked him what the doctor had said that afternoon. Juan Carlos replied that because of an emergency the doctor had had to leave the office for the whole afternoon. At 10:00 he left his house, walked two blocks of dirt streets, and met Nélida. When they had made sure her parents were asleep, they kissed and embraced in the garden. Juan Carlos as usual asked Nélida to give in to him. She refused as usual. Juan Carlos thought of the fact that Nélida was Miss Spring of 1936, kissed her a second time holding her tight, and thought of the tactics that would infallibly seduce her as they had seduced many others. But Juan Carlos did not let his hands go below Nené's waist. He was about to tell her he was no fool, that he only acted the fool: "Hey kid, you're in bad shape, if you don't stop fooling around with dames you're going to kick the bucket, try to reduce the quota, I'm not saying anything more, the next time, as the family doctor, I'm going to tell your old lady." Overwhelmed by an impulse Juan Carlos suddenly took one of her hands and gently brought it down, near his fly, as part of his customary tactics. But then he refrained from making it touch the fly. Nené's hand put up a relative resistance. Juan Carlos hesitated, thought that wild camomile didn't grow in Nené's garden, some said it was poisonous, could it be true? That winter it would be chilly at the door, would he carry out his secret plan before it got cold? every winter night at that door? He thought of a hummingbird who leaves one blossom to go to another, sipping the nectar from all of them, were there drops of nectar in camomile flowers? they seemed dry. He thought of the fact that he was twenty-two and had to take care of himself like an old man. He brusquely let go of Nélida and stepped back toward the hedge. Angrily he pulled off a branch. At 11:20 he thought it necessary to fondle her breasts passing his hand under her blouse and bodice, since he should maintain her interest in him. At 11:30 they said good-night. At 11:46 Juan Carlos passed the construction site of the new police station. There were no lighted windows in the houses on the block, there were no people on the street. A block away he could see a couple walking in his direction. It took five minutes for them to pass, they turned the corner and disappeared. Juan Carlos again looked in all directions, he couldn't see any living being. It was already midnight, the appointed time. His heart began to beat faster, he crossed the street and entered the site. He made his way easier than the night before, remembering the details of the courtyard seen in daylight. He thought that in order to climb the brick wall, three yards high, an old man would need a ladder and wouldn't be able to climb the scaffolds like him. Already on top of the wall he thought that an old man couldn't jump down to the neighboring courtyard. Without knowing why, he remembered the nearly adolescent girl who had looked at him that afternoon, provoking him. He decided to follow her someday, the girl lived on a farm in the outskirts. Juan Carlos wiped the dirt off his hands on his rancher's jacket and prepared to jump.

FIFTH EPISODE

For today's modern woman, personality comes before beauty.

(radio commercial for lipstick,
Buenos Aires, 1937)

The aforementioned Thursday, April 23, 1937, María Mabel Sáenz, known to all as Mabel, opened her eyes at 7:00 A.M. when her Swiss alarm clock rang. She couldn't keep them open and went back to sleep. At 7:15 the cook knocked on her door and told her that breakfast was served. Throughout Mabel's body her nerves felt drowsy, warm, sheathed in honey or jelly, the things she touched, the sounds she heard seemed softer, her skull, pleasantly empty, was full of tepid air. Her sense of smell instead was sharpened, first her nose shuddered at the traces of lime-scented brilliantine on the white linen pillow, the smell then sent shudders down her chest, through to her arms and legs. At 7:25 she had an almost cold cup of coffee alone in the dining room, she didn't want the cook to reheat it, instead she ordered fresh, crunchy toast, which she spread with butter. At 7:46 she entered Public School 1 of the Department of Education for the Province of Buenos Aires. At 7:55 the bell rang to line up in the courtyard. Mabel placed herself at the head of the fifth grade division B students. The principal said "Good morning, children," the students answered her in unison "Good morning, principal." At 8:01 the bell rang again and each line marched to its classroom. In the first hour Mabel gave a his-

59

tory lesson, the subject, the Incas. The recess bell rang three times, at 9:00, 10:00, and 11:00; the last bell rang at exactly noon, at which time classes were over. By then Mabel had carried out her morning plan: to explain new problems in interest, equity, and capital, to avoid carting covered notebooks home by correcting the homework right in class while the students solved supplementary arithmetic problems in their work notebooks, to let Celina know during one of the recesses that she might go to her house after lunch, and to avoid the grown-up students who sat in the back of the classroom. At 12:20 she came home with a big appetite, her mother asked if she could wait until 2:00 to have lunch with her father and possibly with her fiancé Cecil, after the cattle auction. Mabel had a ready answer. The cook boiled some ravioli for her separately and served them with chicken broth. Mabel's mother could not join her because she had to bathe and change clothes, she had been cleaning the house all morning and wasn't used to it. Mabel tried some roast chicken after the ravioli but abstained from dessert. She argued that she needed help from Celina to prepare her language class, if she stayed home she'd have to entertain Cecil for half the afternoon at least, what with lunch and after-dinner liqueur. At 1:45 Mabel entered the Etchepare house without knocking. In keeping with Mabel's request, Celina led her directly into her room. Mabel's eyelids were heavy and with difficulty she listened to Celina's complaints: Juan Carlos was mean to his mother and sister, surely goaded on by Nené, on top of which he didn't take care of himself, the night before he had been out with that nobody until three in the morning, anyone could easily catch tuberculosis that way. Mabel told her that the night before she had slept less than four hours, from waiting on Cecil and her father, so she would gladly stay for siesta right there if it was possible. Celina let her have her bed and lay on some cushions on the floor. Mabel closed her eyes

60

at 2:10 and was still sleeping when the grandfather clock struck 5:00. Celina woke her up and offered her tea. Mabel refused it and rushed home, she had promised to go to the six o'clock show at the movies with her mother. Reaching the corner of her house she saw that her father and Cecil were at the entranceway talking as they walked to the car. Before they could see her Mabel stepped into the corner grocery store. To justify her presence she bought a large box of biscuits; she wavered between her two favorite brands: the one with the picture of French court ladies and the one with the picture of an elegant modern couple in black tie. At 5:15 she entered her house, she had carried out her afternoon plan: to avoid her father who would have made her entertain Cecil, and to sleep a refreshing siesta. Despite their hurry mother and daughter opened the box of biscuits, and at 6:05 entered the Seville movie theater, the only movie house in town, run by the Spanish Aid Society. In the lobby decorated with typical porcelain tiles, Mabel observed the posters of that day's feature and noticed with disappointment that the styles were at least three years behind, which confirmed the fact that American movies took a long time to reach Vallejos. It was a comedy, in the luxurious kind of setting that she loved: spacious drawing rooms with black marble staircases and chrome bannisters, white satin chairs, white satin drapes, fluffy white wool rugs, tables and chairs with chrome legs, where a beautiful New York blonde, a typist, seduces her handsome boss and by means of tricks forces him to divorce his elegant wife. In the end she loses him but finds an old banker who asks for her hand in marriage and takes her to Paris. In the last scene the typist is in front of her Parisian mansion, wrapped in a boa of white feathers, stepping out of a sumptuous white automobile with a white Great Dane, not without first exchanging a look of complicity with the chauffeur, a handsome young man in black boots and uniform. Mabel thought of the intimate relations of the rich ex-typist and the chauffeur, of the possibility that the chauffeur had a bad cold and they decided to make love passionately but without kissing, the superhuman effort to keep from kissing, they can caress but not kiss, in each other's arms all night without being able to get that idea out of their heads, the need to kiss, the promise not to kiss so as to prevent contagion, night after night the same torment, and night after night when carried away with passion their bodies glisten like chrome in the dark, the chrome heart cracks open and the red blood bursts out, overflows, stains the white satin, the white feathers: it's when the chrome can no longer keep back the impetuous blood that their mouths meet every night and present each other with the forbidden kiss. At 7:57 Mabel and her mother came home from the movies. At 8:35 her father and Cecil came in, satisfied with having left everything in order for the auction the next morning, the last of the autumn fair. Cecil gave Mabel a kiss on the cheek. For apéritif they had vermouth. At 9:00 they sat at the table. They ate sardines with potatoes and mayonnaise and then Portuguese veal, cheeses, and ice cream. Her father and Cecil did most of the talking, discussing the morning's sales, and the next day's possibilities, trying to estimate a general balance for the week. When it was time for coffee and cognac they moved toward the living room chairs, but her father suddenly mentioned his doubts about the price on Hereford bulls and dragged Cecil off to the study. Mabel brought them their coffee cups and cognac glasses. She and her mother sat in the living room and discussed the movie. At 10:30 Mabel and Cecil were left alone in the living room, sitting on the same sofa. Cecil kissed her tenderly several times and caressed the back of her neck. He talked about how tired he was, about relaxing on his ranch when the fair was over, about the history books recently arrived from England that he would read: his favorite reading was all that related to English history. He left at 11:05 after drinking three cognacs while sitting with Mabel, added to the two he had in the study, the two vermouths before dinner, and the three glasses of wine emptied during the meal. Mabel exhaled a sigh of relief and looked to see if the door to her parents' bedroom was open. It was closed. She took the bottle of cognac to her room and hid it under the pillow. She returned to the dining room, opened the sideboard and took out two cognac glasses, which joined the hidden bottle. She went to the bathroom and freshened her makeup. She applied her most treasured French perfume. She put on her chaste batiste nightgown with short sleeves, got out two magazines, opened the window slightly, rearranged bottle and glasses, and got into bed. At 11:37 she was comfortably settled and ready to look through the magazines *Feminine World* and *Elegant Paris*. She began with the latter. She quickly skipped the pages corresponding to sport and street wear, continued thinking about Cecil; she was alarmed, the minutes spent in his company seemed longer and longer. Further on the cocktail fashions appeared. Mabel studied them but couldn't get interested in this either. On the next page a small article caught her attention: the language of perfume. The French specialist recommended cool lavenders for the morning, they would revive a man's interest in a woman; for the early afternoon —when visiting museums with an occasional pause for tea —sweeter fragrances, creating the enchantment that would grow at cocktail hour—followed by a candlelight dinner at a night club—already under the rule of another extract, balmy with musk, the aroma of a balcony laden with jasmine upon which yesteryear's *femme fatale* stepped out, fleeing the lights and intrigues of mundane drawing rooms, the same aroma today condensed in a drop of Empire Nocturne, the perfume for today's modern woman. Collections of furs and fine accouterments followed. Mabel stopped at a floor-length black dress, with a full skirt bordered in silver fox. She remembered that in the future Cecil wanted to organize formal receptions at his ranch. Those pages ended with an article on matching furs and jewels. They recommended for light mink aquamarines or amethysts, with chinchilla diamonds only, and for dark brown mink emerald rings and earrings, preferably cut in large rectangles. Mabel read this last article twice. She decided to bring up the subject of jewelry one day in front of Cecil. She thought of the fact that Cecil didn't have a sister and that his mother would someday die in the house in North Cumberland, England. She looked at her alarm clock, it was 11:52. She turned off the light, got up, opened the window, and looked in the direction of the fig tree. The courtyard was deep in total darkness.

The aforementioned Thursday, April 23, 1937, Francisco Catalino Páez, also known as Pancho, woke up at 5:30 A.M. as usual, although the day had not yet dawned. He did not own an alarm clock. There was a new moon and the sky was black, in the lot behind their shack was a water pump. He wet his face and hair, he rinsed his mouth. He always slept without an undershirt because it bothered him, the air outside was cold and he went into the room to put on overalls. His two sisters were sleeping in a big bed, his brother in a corner on a canvas cot. Pancho's bed had springs and a burlap mattress. The shack had a dirt floor, adobe walls, tin roof. His parents slept in the only other room with their youngest son, seven years old. Pancho was the oldest boy. The kitchen was under construction. Pancho had begun it with modern building materials, secondhand. He lit the coal in the stove and prepared boiled maté with milk. He looked for bread, couldn't find it. He awakened his mother; at the bottom of a sack of pumpkins two biscuits had been hidden for Pancho. The biscuits were white, made of flour and fat, Pancho's teeth were big and square, but stained, from the salty pump water. He thought that Juan Carlos had probably just fallen asleep, and could sleep until noon, but he wasn't healthy and Pancho was. He thought of the school mistress who had to get up at 7:00 without having slept, Juan Carlos said she was the prettiest girl in town, especially in a bathing suit. But she was a brunette. The other one was blond, however, and fair. His mother asked him if the biscuits had a damp smell. Pancho said they didn't and looked at her dark Indian skin, the dirt-colored hair, straight, rebellious, streaked with gray. From the wire fence around the club Pancho had seen Mabel in a bathing suit, but she was a brunette. The other one had white legs, sometimes she went to the store without stockings on. Pancho passed a thick comb through his bush of curly black hair, the comb got stuck. His mother told him that he had thick hair like hers, like the Indians, and curly like his Valencian father's. But he couldn't have gotten black eyes from his Indian ancestors, rather from the Moors who had occupied Valencia centuries ago. His mother asked him to make a muscle and then felt his arm, her son wasn't very tall but he was strong all right, without knowing why she thought of the bear cubs in a circus that had passed through Vallejos, and handed him another cup of boiled maté with milk. Pancho thought of the fact that Nené rested the whole night, that her room was next to her parents', and that nobody could enter without being noticed. Pancho thought of the girls at the Gaucho Inn General Store; behind the water pump the wooden fence that separated his family's lot from the neighbor's looked rundown, black with moss. Without knowing why Pancho sought for something else to look at, in the east the sun was coming out, up above there were red clouds, then pink ones and yellow ones nearer the sun, and behind it the yellow sky, but the shack covered the opposite horizon which was still black, then blue, and when Pancho set out for the construction site of the new police station one horizon was as sky-blue as the other. Some women from the neighboring shacks were already up, sweeping courtyards or drinking maté. The other girl didn't have stiff hair growing out from her forehead: her hair was soft, blond, with amazing natural curls; she didn't have fuzz on her cheeks, over her upper lip, on her chin: her skin was white and shiny; her eyebrows were not joined like an owl's and the whites of her eyes yellowish: her eyebrows were barely two arched threads, her eyes—light blue?—and her nose a little hooked but her lips were rosy; she wasn't short and stocky: she was as tall as him, her waist would almost completely fit into his big bricklayer's hands, moving up, her waist widened to where her white bust protruded, moving down, her waist widened into hips, and didn't blondes have pubic hair? in the Gaucho Inn there was a bleached blonde but her pubic hair was dark: Pancho without knowing why imagined Nené asleep with her legs slightly apart, without pubic hair, like a little girl, and in the summer she always went to the store without stockings on; Nené didn't use espadrilles: her feet were sheathed in high-heel shoes; she didn't perspire: she didn't have to rub herself like the maids; Nené wasn't a coarse Indian woman: she talked like a radio speaker and she enunciated all her words. At 6:45 Pancho was at the construction site. The foreman ordered him and two other bricklayers to unload a truck full of bricks and to cart them over to the courtyard where the offices of the low-ranking personnel were to be built. At 8:07 the foreman ordered him to dig an L-shaped pit by the back wall. Pancho had to force the shovel, his companions laughed and said he had hit upon tosca, the rockiest kind of soil on the pampas. Nené's white legs, the dark thighs of the girls at the Gaucho Inn, Mabel's black pubic hair, Big Fanny's dark backside, Nené, Big Fanny, Nené's white, hairless pubis; the tosca dust was sticking to his nostrils and going down his throat. At 11:45 the foreman clanged a pole against an old pan as the signal to break for lunch. Pancho washed his face under the faucet and fought his rough tangles with his comb. Before going home he took a circuitous route around two blocks to pass Doctor Nastini's house. Big Fanny was nowhere to be seen. Pancho walked eleven blocks to his house. His eldest sister served him potatoes, pumpkin, and meat stew for lunch. Pancho asked how her rheumatism was doing, said that she should let him know when she could go back to work, he would talk to both the builder and the owner of the brick oven about getting her a job as a maid. At 1:25 Pancho returned to the construction site. The foreman did not look at his watch and ordered him to continue with the pit before it was time. Pancho did not have a watch and obeyed, he was sure it wasn't time to begin but he took the shovel and drove it into the rocky soil. He thought of the fact that the foreman had spoken well of him to the builder and the chief of police. At 2:35 the foreman relieved him and sent him to the old police station to get one of the jail bars just arrived from Buenos Aires and being stored at the police lieutenant's office. Pancho got up the nerve and spoke to the police lieutenant about his aim to become a police officer. The lieutenant replied that they needed able-bodied boys like him, but that he'd have to save up for the six-month course at La Plata, the provincial capital. Pancho asked if you had to pay for the course. The official made it clear that the course was free and that he would receive room and board during the six months without salary, but the Vallejos police force could only send candidates if it received permission from the capital, everything depended on the capital. Pancho carried the bar out pretending that it was no effort. Afraid that the police lieutenant might go out on the sidewalk and watch him he covered two blocks without stopping to rest. At 4:32 he joyously received a visit from his friend Juan Carlos. At 4:45 the foreman clanged the pan again. Pancho looked at Juan Carlos's face, looking for signs of illness and signs of recovery. At a table in the tavern Pancho told him to be careful not to get caught in somebody else's house, why didn't he settle for Nené? Juan Carlos said that as soon as he got what he was after, there would be no more Nené, and asked Pancho to swear not to tell anyone: Mabel had promised to convince the Englishman to take him on as the manager of both ranches. Juan Carlos added that one owner can't be at two ranches at the same time, and being the manager is like being the owner of one of the two. Pancho asked him if he would continue with Nené in the event that he got that job. Juan Carlos replied that he asked that question because he didn't know anything about women. Pancho wanted to learn but pretended to make fun of it all. Juan Carlos said that Nené was like all the rest, if one treated her nice she acted up, if one treated her bad she stayed in line. The important thing was to make Mabel jealous so that she wouldn't forget to do him that favor. At 6:23 Pancho washed at the shack under the jet of cold water from the pump. At 7:05 his mother and older sister walked in slowly and laboriously. His sister had felt a lot of pain in her waist that afternoon and both had gone to the hospital to ask for some medicine. The doctor had again told them that it was rheumatism resulting from the five years she had worked as a laundress with her arms in cold water, that she could go back to work but not as a laundress, and that she should stay away from water as much as possible. At 8:05 the stew from lunch was already reheated and they all ate together. Pancho hardly spoke and at 8:30 he went out for a slow walk toward the center of town. His companions from the construction site would be at the tavern. He thought of the disadvantage of police officials seeing him at the tavern. He thought of the advantage of them seeing him in the company of Juan Carlos, a government employee. A girl came out of the Italian poulterer's farm carrying two plucked chickens. It was Big Fanny. He walked faster and caught up with her as if by chance. They were walking almost side by side. Pancho said good evening respectfully. Big Fanny answered back the same. Pancho asked her how much the Italian charged for chickens. Big Fanny answered in a low voice and added that she had to walk faster since her mistress was waiting for her. Pancho asked if she would allow him to walk her as far as the corner of the nuns' school. Big Fanny said a hesitating yes and then no. Pancho walked her and found out that on Sunday evening Big Fanny would go to the country fair taking place at the Spanish Meadow, celebrating the season's close. Carrying out his friend's order, Pancho advised her to change employers and go work at the Sáenz house. Fanny answered that it wasn't nice to desert her employer. On the corner of the nuns' school, Pancho considered the possibility of walking the two miles of empty lots to the Gaucho Inn General Store. He wanted to see his girlfriends there, close his eyes, and think of someone else. But it was too far to go alone, with Juan Carlos he would have. It wasn't that he had no money, as he had lied to his friend. He picked up a eucalyptus branch lying on the ground, it was flexible, holding it by its two ends Pancho bent the branch slightly, the fiber yielded, Pancho increased the pressure, the fiber yielded but began to creak. The branch wasn't tough like the bricks, it was soft; it wasn't heavy like the bar from the lieutenant's office, it was light; the branch had lost its brown bark and the smooth surface glowed light green, Pancho increased the pressure of his arms, the fiber creaked, Pancho slackened the bough slightly and then pressed it again decisively, the fiber creaked once more and split in two. At 9:47 Pancho was back home. They were all huddled in his mother's room listening to a tango singer on the radio. Pancho was sleepy and didn't join the

69

family. He went to bed, thinking that his sister would have a hard time getting a job as a maid if she couldn't put her hands in water to wash clothes or dishes and the six months without salary in the province's capital would be a long time. He looked at his brother's cot that had no mattress. He thought of the fact that his bed had both springs and a burlap mattress; it had cost him more than a month's salary, on a whim he had refused to buy a secondhand bed. He regretted having spent so much, but his brother slept in a cot and he didn't. A few minutes later he was asleep.

The aforementioned Thursday, April 23, 1937, Antonia Josefa Ramírez, also called Big Fanny by some, and by others Fanny, woke up to the chirping of the birds nested in the carob tree in the courtyard. The first thing she saw was the heap of objects stored in her room: bottles of bleach, jugs of wine, cans of oil, a cask of port wine, strings of garlic hanging from the wall, sacks of potatoes, onions, cans of kerosene, and bars of soap. Her bedroom was also a pantry. Instead of a bathroom she had to make do with an old outhouse and the laundry sink, at the rear of the courtyard. There, at 6:35, she washed her face, neck, and armpits. Then she applied the reddish antiperspirant that the mistress had bought for her. Before putting on her gray long-sleeved apron she fluttered her arms like a bird so that the red drops would dry: the mistress had told her that otherwise they would burn her clothes. She lit the wood-burning stove and had a cup of coffee with milk, bread and butter. She washed the doctor's undershirts, underpants, and shirts until 7:45. She awakened the mistress and prepared breakfast for the Nastinis and their children. She set the table in the dinette connected to the kitchen. She prepared toast. She washed the breakfast dishes. She swept and dusted the doctor's office, the waiting room, the children's bedroom, the master bedroom, the living room, the dining room, and finally the sidewalk. She was interrupted twice by the mistress: she had to go to the butcher to pick up the order made by phone, and to the grocery store to get grating cheese. One of the children spilled a glass of milk in the parlor and the mistress suggested that she take the opportunity to scrub the tile floor and give it a quick layer of wax. At 11:30 the mistress caused another interruption by asking Fanny to set the table for lunch while she took a bath. At 12:00 the mistress and her two children, a boy and a girl, sat at the table. At 12:30 the three left for school where the mistress was a teacher and the children studied. Meanwhile Fanny washed the bathroom, equipped with all the modern conveniences. At 1:10 the doctor came home from the hospital and Fanny served him the meal the mistress had prepared for him. The doctor looked at her legs and as usual Fanny avoided coming near him. At 1:45 Fanny sat at the table and ate the generous leftovers from lunch. At 3:06 she finished washing the dishes and cleaning the kitchen. The tasks to be done when the doctor was at home were the most tiresome because she couldn't accompany herself singing, while in the morning she'd sing many different songs, usually milongas and tangos, heard in the movies starring her favorite singing actress. She refreshed herself with water in the sink out back and lay down to rest. She thought about the mistress's advice. According to Mrs. Nastini, housemaids shouldn't let boys from another social class walk them home or have more than one dance at the country fairs. Above all, housemaids should keep away from students, bank clerks, traveling salesmen, store owners, and store salesmen. It was well known that they were in the habit of going steady with girls from good families—"and behaving like perfect angels, Fanny"— and later, in the dark, they would try and seduce housemaids, who were the easiest prey because of their ignorance. Mrs. Nastini forgot to include married men on the list. She recommended instead any good hardworking boy, words which indicated any blue-collar worker. Fanny thought about the Argentine movie she had seen the Friday before, starring her favorite singing actress, the story of a maid in a boarding house who falls in love with one of the boarders, a law student. How had she managed to make him fall in love with her? The girl had suffered a lot to succeed in her quest and Fanny realized a very important point: the girl had never planned to make him fall in love, he had begun to like her because she was evidently good and self-sacrificing, to the point of passing for the mother of another unmarried girl's baby, the daughter of the boarding house's proprietress. Later on the student got his law degree and defended her before justice, since the maid wanted to keep the baby who wasn't hers, already feeling a mother's love, but everything came out all right in the end. Fanny decided that if someone from a higher social class proposed marriage to her one day she wouldn't be a fool and reject him, but neither would she be the one to look for it. Besides, there were many good hardworking boys whom she liked: Minguito the bread delivery boy, Aureliano the farmer, Pancho the bricklayer, Chiche the newspaper boy. But maybe the next day she couldn't go to the movies as usual at the popular Friday prices, because her employers had guests for dinner. Without knowing why Fanny picked up an espadrille from the floor and threw it forcibly against a shelf. A bottle of bleach fell and broke. Fanny picked up the pieces, dried the floor and returned to bed. At 4:00 she got up and set the table for the mistress's and the children's snack. She called the elderly lady who helped as the doctor's nurse and offered her the usual cup of tea. At 5:28 she finished washing the snack dishes and went across the street to the Argentine Bargain Store to pick up the dishtowels the mistress had ordered. Nené asked her how the new nurse treated her, they had already had three since she left. Fanny thought of her old school bench, she used to sit in the fourth row with the present maid at the mayor's house, in the second row Nené with Kela Rodríguez, in the first row Mabel Sáenz and Celina Etchepare. Mabel and Kela would soon be married. Would Celina's brother marry Nené despite her business with Nastini? Before, Nené used to give her old clothes. How many people in Vallejos knew what had happened? Fanny thought of asking Nené for some more old things. Nené had given her so many pretty secondhand clothes, and had she shown her gratitude? But Celina had promised to recommend her to Mabel's mother to take her on as a maid, they had a cook already and she would have less work, and Doctor Nastini wouldn't be looking at her legs. The recess bell would ring and Mabel, Celina, and Nené would run to play jump rope, one, two, three, four, a hundred jumps before the next bell. Nené did the package of dishtowels and looked at her but they didn't talk as before. Yes, Nené had recommended her to the Nastinis, they had taken her on thanks to the nurse, thanks to Nené, thanks to her old schoolmate who had given her how many used garments? a sweater, a dress, a shawl, shoes, when Nené used to work for Doctor Nastini. Fanny left the store without asking the packer for old clothes. At 5:50 she began to iron the shirts washed that morning. At 7:53 she set the table for dinner which the mistress had prepared. At 8:21 she went to the poulterer's farm to fetch the chickens they were sending the doctor as a gift. At 8:41 Pancho the bricklayer approached her and talked to her. Fanny tried to hide her enthusiasm. Pancho was wearing a shirt with short sleeves that revealed two hairy muscular arms, the neck was open, and you could see that his chest was covered with the same thick hair. Without knowing why Fanny thought of a ferocious gorilla, sporting thick but well-delineated eyebrows, curled eyelashes, and a mustache partially covering his large mouth.

The mistress would not be angry if she danced with him at the fairs. Fanny walked beside the bricklayer, touching up her hair from time to time, Fanny's hair began halfway down her forehead, straight, thick, and dirt colored. At 8:52 she passed the Seville movie theater alone, it announced the next day's show, at the popular Friday prices, an Argentine comedy. Despite the fact they weren't showing a movie with her favorite singing actress, she would still go to the show with the mayor's maid, just like every Friday, five cents for ladies and ten for gentlemen, but what if the dinner guests were late and she couldn't go to the movies? It almost didn't matter anymore, and what about her half-day off Sunday? At the fair there would be Pancho who had already expressed his desire to have a few dances with her. Without knowing why Fanny thought of the birds in the courtyard's carob tree, they were probably cuddled together in their nest at that moment, warm and cozy. She felt like being warm and cozy in her bed already; one cold night the mistress had come into her room, to get port wine from the cask for her husband's friends, and upon seeing Fanny in bed the mistress had asked if she needed another blanket. Fanny felt like being warm and cozy in her bed, if the mistress came into her room tonight she would tell her about having met Pancho on the street. At 9:20 she sat down to eat the leftovers from dinner. At 10:15 she finished washing the dishes and the kitchen. Fanny thought that the day had been easy, no curtains to wash or wood floors to scrape. At 10:25 the doctor asked her to buy a pack of cigarettes for him at the bar. At 11:02 she went to bed and thought that if she married Pancho she would settle for living in a one-room house with a tin roof, but she would refuse to store objects that didn't belong in the bedroom: she would have Pancho at least build a wing for storing bottles of bleach, jugs, casks, sacks of potatoes, strings of garlic, and cans of kerosene. Suddenly she remembered that Pancho was friends with Celina's brother, and Celina's brother was going steady with Nené. She thought of the fact that she had not been fair to Nené, she hadn't kept her promise. Fanny clasped her hands and asked for God's forgiveness. She remembered Nené's words: "if you do wrong by me God will punish you."

SIXTH EPISODE

> Your tangos are fatherless children,
> roaming the streets at dark,
> when each of the doors is bolted
> and ghosts of song dismally bark.
>
> (from H. Manzi's tango "Malena")

Temporary Gypsy Camp, Vallejos, Saturday,
April 25, 1937

I don't know you, you come here and this poor gypsy woman tells you everything, for one peso. But you send all your friends to me, because I always guess right. Now I tell your past, present, and future   Just the future? then I tell you just the future: when the young dogs drop in they always ask me about the present though, at least the part about their cuties loving them or not. But you're so good-looking you don't care, eh? you've got her wrapped around your finger   For the same price, but I can't tell you, you're handsome all right but my you're in a hurry, you've got to wait for the cards to tell you. And you're not worried if she loves you or not anyway, you're thinking a guy like you is hard to find, you pretty boys are all alike. And in death you're not interested either because you're young and healthy, so I bet all you want to know is if there's money up ahead, all the money you ever wanted. How do you like that, I guessed it even before dealing your cards, haven't I? But before I read your future tell me if you want to know everything or just the good parts   Such a pretty boy in such an expensive leather jacket and you're not going to give this poor gypsy fifty cents more? that way I tell you the good and the bad   Cut, with your left hand   Now cut again, still with your left hand, in three parts, so you've got the past, present, and future, and now we turn the cards over and we have . . . the King of Diamonds, and he doesn't want to give us a smile, he's looking rather cross, see how his crown is pulled down over his eyes so it won't fall off, and his velvet cape is heavy on him but it keeps him warm—a dark man, kind of old already, who doesn't love you, he's doing you harm, what you want most in life which if I'm not mistaken is . . . hard cash, is what he's not going to give you—and next to him the Queen of Spades is also looking rather cross, she's real angry, see how she's holding out her hand to you, she's going to give you something, but be careful because she has a strange look about her, all wrapped in that gold-embroidered rag, it's a red rag but look: on her sleeves you can see the violet lining for a wake, and her hair—not blond, nor brunette, nor red, do you know any bald lady? I don't see her hair . . . and luckily next to her is the Three of Spades, see how pointy those tips look, their silver handles are on your side—which means you're going on a journey by land—do you know any woman with bleached hair or with a wig who recently took a trip? help me because I can't seem to understand why she's bald   Yes, I know the card shows black hair but she looked bald to me just when you cut the deck   If you don't know any bald lady then you're the one who's traveling, you're going on a journey, to save yourself from the fate the old man and the bald dame are preparing for you. If she had no eyes I'd say it was Misfortune who was running after you and who's going to catch you, she doesn't care if you're old, young, or just a baby, or handsome or ugly, Misfortune is blind, but it's strange for the Queen of Diamonds to come out bald. Let me shuffle and don't you go looking at the cards while I mix them because that makes the dead cry. You know who the dark old man is?   Then the father of the girl you're going out with doesn't want you in the house, and the Bald Lady is helping him, is the girl blond or brunette?   Are you sure she doesn't bleach her hair black or wear a black wig?   Now cut again into three parts, with your left hand   Two of Clubs, the two black clovers, they're not four leafed though, they don't bring you good luck—someone's going to betray you, it's not the old man nor the Bald Lady—and it's next to the Ace of Clubs, poor thing it has no decorations, like this miserable tent, it's a poor card but a good one—yes, the one you least expect is going to play a dirty trick on you, but when you're down and out you're going to realize that every cloud has a silver lining—and here's a blonde who loves you: the Queen of Hearts, she has a flower for you in her right hand—hey, she brings you luck, but just be careful, I don't like blondes, this is just for the record, it has nothing to do with the cards, but blondes have fair flesh so that you'll think they have fair hearts too, she puts her heart in your hand, you're going to look at it, wait, what I see is that she tears it out and gives it to you, never let go of the blonde's rotten heart, keep a firm grasp on it! a spirit told me that a blonde's heart once broke like an egg and out came an ugly bird—but even though the little Queen's a blonde she's going to help you, the cards say so, but I don't like her   No, the lifeline comes afterward, you've got to wait for the last cut and then choose thirteen cards. But now cut again into three, like before   The Five of Hearts, marriage! send me some wedding cake, honey, but I'm not sure you're the one who's been hooked, it's just as well because when I touched the card it felt cold, there's no joy in that wedding, there's no joy in a cold card, the wedding will be sad because the wine is going to spill, it's going to fall to the floor, what a pity because I like wine, honey, it's good for the health, but when it spills on the floor it smells awful. Are you the one who's getting married? no, because next to it comes an old woman, the Queen of Clubs, who's on your side, she looks prepared to protect you, she's going to keep you warm with that silver- and gold-embroidered cape she's wearing, how the gypsy king would like that cape, honey, all he has you know are these dirty tents, and here's the Six of Diamonds   No, honey, the Six of Diamonds means dough when it comes up alone, but next to this Queen it's the dead who get the dough, the only thing you're left with is Sincerity   How do you like the six little diamonds, you think they're precious stones, don't you? but when they're next to a queen or a knave it means the queen or the knave is doing good by you, they don't give you money because they don't have much, what they can give you is sincerity, which is the diamond of the spirit   No, it's not your mother, this one's old but she doesn't love you like a son, but she's good, my but you have dames coming out of every corner, honey, it must be the jacket, or is it the hanger, eh honey? you're quite a knockout aren't you, you wouldn't like to join the circus, would you? I know you wouldn't . . . but listen, if you did . . . the king would marry us immediately, and this I'm telling you for the heck of it, okay? now cut again   Now this time I am going to draw your lifeline, pick out thirteen of these scattered cards, but don't turn them over ahead of time because the dead aren't going to like you, there was a gypsy girl who turned the cards over and the dead put poison in her food, because when a living person turns a card over ahead of time . . . a dead person can fall from heaven   Yes, he falls into hell, because if you turn a card ahead of time a dead man is tempted and looks down from heaven and sees on earth the naked body of someone bathing and gets bad sinful thoughts again and the saints throw him down to hell, and he burns there on account of you   Now you can start turning them over, one after the other. The Five of Spades is Gossip, evil tongues cut like a spade's edge, they cut and chop to pieces—but what do you care, the Five of Spades kills women, while the more they talk about you the better, right?—and the Two of Diamonds is an engagement— it's the first time I see you're going to fall in love, because not one love card has come up so far, disgusting pig, so many dames and you don't love any—but I don't see the one you're going to love, she doesn't seem to be any of the ones who have come up so far, and if she's one of those dames, honey, life sure has changed her, I don't recognize her

No, the Two of Diamonds isn't money either, it's an engagement, the two diamonds are two souls, both the same, not the two precious stones that you'd prefer—no! honey, why did you pick such a terrible card? the Four of Spades is serious sickness, but if a Queen or a Knave or a King comes up next you're saved, wait, let me touch a little gypsy dust, and you too touch this dust in the little pouch, now turn the next card over . . . honey, the Four of Diamonds is tears, but maybe you can save yourself yet, maybe the tears are for somebody else, hurry, make up your mind and turn another   I'm telling you no, the only diamond cards that mean money are the Nine and Ten, and you're not drawing those, if some gypsy told you otherwise she was talking through her hat so that you'd walk out happy, but you asked me to tell you the good and the bad. Now shut up and turn the next card   The Knave of Clubs! you're saved, take the dagger out of my heart, honey, it's for saving you that I might get the Misfortune and the Tears, throw a bit of that dust on my neck and shoulders, let me open my dress, quick . . . what's so disgusting? . . . don't tell me you're the demon the dead Snailtail had predicted would visit me, pass me those ashes quick   What do you care if they're ashes, what do you care if they're human ashes, they're bitch-dog ashes . . . thanks . . . thanks, honey, you see the dead Snailtail told me to watch out for demons, they can get into my tent by entering you without you realizing it, it can happen to anyone   Sickness? which? yes, let me look, the Four of Spades, but it may be a dark fellow who gets it, the Knave of Clubs—a very strong man, he's not a bad man—turn the next card . . . the Six of Hearts, look at those little hearts, all the same size, all red with blood, but when I touched the card it was colder than the others! it's the card of kisses, caresses, madly passionate love, but the card was cold when I touched it, it must be that woman who betrays you, but I don't understand anything now, turn the next card over . . . the Magpie!! no, no, don't show me your death, but wait, is it your death? . . . beware because someone dies a violent death, the Nine of Spades after cold hearts means someone dies screaming, is there anyone who wants to kill you? turn the next card . . . again the Queen of Diamonds! but this time she doesn't look angry   What do you mean she hasn't come up? she did come up! the Bald Lady, I told you she's pursuing you   You're right, it was the Queen of Spades, I'm getting old, you see honey, that's why you don't love me . . . then what's this Queen of Diamonds? She doesn't look dark, and she's not bad, but if you're lucky she's the one who's going to give up the ghost, quick the next card! the Eight of Spades . . . and it's in the first, third, fifth, ninth place: the worst place of all, the most dangerous, look at me, sweetheart, I want to look deep into your eyes to see if I can understand something, sometimes I have to look into a pitcher of water, or wine, or into glass, anything I can use as a mirror, I don't know . . . but that's a lot of nasty cards in a row, if the Eight of Spades had come after a club you'd be saved, completely, but the bad streak still hasn't ended, let me look into your eyes, I like light brown eyes, but I don't see anything in them, I just see myself, ah, honey, if you only knew how pretty I once was, when a young dog like you would come into my tent I'd always make sure there was another gypsy woman right outside on guard in case I screamed, they all felt tempted to put their hands on me! . . . draw another card, and don't forget that someone suffers a violent death, beware, stay away from danger, I see blood and I hear the scream of someone fatally wounded, draw another card . . . finally, a good one, the Seven of Hearts is happiness, you will have great joy after all those troubles, turn one more! . . . the Three of Spades, again the journey   No, silly, not the journey to the next world, it's a journey by land and not a long one, and it's going to go well for you, another card now, there's only two to go! . . . the Five of Hearts, and it's the warmest I've touched in the whole deck, it's a good card always, it means that you're going to do a lot of talking with someone, and you're going to agree on something, it's already the next to the last card, my handsome cherub, it means that you're going to be a happy old man, you're going to be in good company, and now cherub touch the ashes, put the tips of the five fingers of your right hand into the pouch . . . because the last card is tough . . . choose . . . turn it over   The Queen of Clubs! the old woman! . . . and she came up again after a good hearts card, that's nice, honey, it means you're going to die an old man beside your wife who will be old like you, because the Queen of Clubs is an old woman, like me   Are you satisfied? does one peso fifty seem a lot for telling your whole little fortune?   No, I'm the one to thank you, send me your friends now, and may they all be like you, spark of heavenly flame that quits this mortal frame . . . .

. . . .

A bald Queen of Spades, did some bitch-dog of mine die bald? the burnt bitch had hair, the poor little chunk of coal, the little old pile of ash, and the Bald Woman is either a lie told by a pregnant pigeon who isn't pregnant, or it's some bad pigeon's revenge . . . no, her bald noggin is cold, a bald noggin doesn't have hair to keep it nice and warm, a bald noggin doesn't love anybody, like the young dog, that one didn't want to stay with me because he doesn't love anybody, not me nor any of the others, his noggin seems healthy but it's spoiled, all rotten inside . . . that's it, the noggin was healthy but the devil made her open her mouth and then spit inside, the stupid Queen doesn't know the devil's spit is pus . . . and all her hair fell out.

Country fair, Sunday, April 26, 1937, in the Spanish Meadow: Its Course and Denouement

Opening time: 6:30 P.M.
Price of tickets: one peso for the gentlemen, twenty cents for the ladies.
First dance performed by the musical band called Los Armónicos: tango "Don Juan."
Lady most admired in the course of the evening: Raquel Rodríguez.
Prevailing perfume: that which emanated from the leaves of the eucalyptus trees surrounding the Spanish Meadow.
Ornament most worn by the ladies: a silk ribbon placed as a headband to heighten permanent waves.
Flower most frequently chosen by the gentlemen to place in the buttonhole of their lapels: the carnation.
Most appreciated dance: waltz "From My Soul."
Fastest dance: paso doble "El relicario."
Slowest dance: habanera "You."

High point of the evening: the presence of eighty-two couples on the dance floor during the performance of the waltz "From My Soul."

Greatest alarm suffered by those present: gust of wind at 9:04 falsely portending an imminent downpour.

Signal to indicate the termination of the evening: two brief blackouts, at 11:30.

Closing time: 11:45.

Lady with the most hopes of all those present: Antonia Josefa Ramírez, also known as Big Fanny or Fanny.

Fanny's companion: her best friend, the mayor's housemaid.

Fanny's first dance of the evening: ranchera "My Little Ranch," paired off with Mister Domingo Gilano, also known as Minguito.

Gentleman who attended the fair with the intention of breaking into Fanny's existence: Franciso Catalino Páez, also known as Pancho.

Fanny and Pancho's first dance: tango "The Man from Entre Rios."

Fanny and Pancho's first dance cheek to cheek: habanera "You."

Drinks Fanny consumed and Pancho paid for: two orangeades.

Condition imposed by Pancho in order to talk to her about a matter of great importance to them both: that she let him take her home without the presence of her girlfriend.

Condition imposed by Fanny: that they first take her friend home to the mayor's house, from where she and Pancho, alone, would proceed to Doctor Nastini's house.

Place Fanny designated for the conversation: the front door of Doctor Nastini's residence.

Circumstance which displeased Pancho: the fact that the mayor's house was in the paved and well-lighted section of town, only two blocks from Doctor Nastini's residence, already far from the wooded and dark zone of dirt streets where the Spanish Meadow was located.

Lady who was worried at seeing Fanny go off in Pancho's company in the direction of the Nastini residence: the mayor's housemaid.

Barometric circumstances which facilitated the fulfillment of Pancho's intentions: the pleasantly cool temperature, 61 degrees Fahrenheit, and the new moon.

Chance circumstance which facilitated said intentions: the approach of a ferocious-looking stray dog who frightened Fanny and gave rise to an unmistakable show of courage on the part of Pancho, which awakened in Fanny a warm sense of security.

Another chance circumstance: the existence of a construction site in the vicinity, which could be reached by wandering just one block off the direct route.

Important matter Pancho spoke to Fanny about, as promised: his desire to be with her, a desire which in his words obsessed him night and day.

Reason of which Pancho availed himself to make Fanny pass the construction site of the new police station: the necessity to talk a while longer, and not at the front door of Doctor Nastini's residence, to avoid possible slander.

Pancho's prevailing thoughts while with Fanny in the dark: tall grass, the weeds that must be cut, the foreman's coming for sure, go grab a shovel Pancho, hoe the weeds, it's dark and not even a cat can see us, Juan Carlos jumps from the brick wall, he doesn't go into the weeds, "when you're with a chick in a place where nobody can see you, don't waste any time talking, where will that get you? in trouble, that's where," the roots of the weeds in the soil split by drought, the soil is all dust, from the middle of your forehead this tough dirt-colored hair grows, one yank at the weeds and I pull them out by the roots, a hairy root with clods of dirt, weeds don't grow on the tosca soil, Fanny's hair is nicer than the roots of the weeds, you can touch it, without any clod of dirt, how nice and clean Fanny is, she has brown arms and her legs are even browner, does she have hairy legs? no, just a little bit of fuzz, the packer goes to the store without stockings and Nené's skin must be nice and soft when you touch it, you really don't want to be kissed? she doesn't even know how to kiss, she has a little mustache, dark gams, dark face, can I caress you just a bit? so soft poor little dark girl, I pass the bricks to the next worker, we take two, three bricks off the truck at a time and they scrape my hands as I pass them, they're as dry as tosca soil, "we must take your fingerprints," and the finger smeared on the enrollment book didn't make a mark at all, "you don't have fingerprints anymore, the bricks have swallowed them up," only on my pinky, the laziest of all the fingers, I caress you and you're smooth, "if you don't rope her in, she'll take you for a fool," I'm going to tell her that I love her really and truly, maybe she'll believe it, I'll tell her she's very pretty, that they've told me she's hardworking, that she keeps her mistress's house clean, what more can I tell a housemaid? as meek as a lamb she is, and she doesn't know from nothing, I feel bad about putting one over on her, "if you don't grab her . . . ," she thinks I'm in love with her, she thinks that I'll marry her tomorrow, her little mustache is just soft fuzz, I carried the bar more than two blocks, if I want I can squeeze and break you, see how strong I can be, but not to hit you, it's to protect you from dogs, she's meek as a little lamb, but if you get bullheaded you're a goner just the same, see how strong I can be . . .

Fanny's prevailing thoughts while with Pancho in the dark: the mistress can't see me, I won't tell my friend about it, I didn't dance with those fellows from the bank, I didn't dance with the students ma'm, I didn't dance with the kind you told me never to dance with, Pancho's not the kind who takes advantage of the maids after going steady with the others, just a good hardworking boy, the mistress doesn't have to beg me to go and work, I grab hold of the broom with my two hands and sweep the floor, I dust the furniture with the feather duster, with a wet rag and soap I wash the floors, the soap and the scrubbing board are kept in the kitchen sink, he bought a gentleman's ticket for one peso, the orangeade was so refreshing, and I came as a lady and paid only twenty cents, the girls who go to the dance buy ladies' tickets even though they're only maids, the same as the store clerks, dressmakers' assistants, or young ladies who are teachers, he has callouses on his hands, those hard callouses give me chills, my he did send that dog packing! if the doctor tries to take advantage of me one day I'll run and call for Pancho, he forgot to put stays in his collar and the two tips curl up, when I see him again I'll give him some of the doctor's stays, ay what a nice chill, what hard kisses he gives me, is it true that he loves me? it gives me goose pimples when he kisses me so hard and caresses me so slowly . . .

New feelings experienced by Fanny the night of April 26, 1937, when saying good-night to Pancho at the street door of Doctor Nastini's residence: the desire to see Pancho on some dark sidewalk the next night, without stays in his shirt collar so that she could put in his shirt the ones appropriated from Doctor Nastini.

Route of Fanny's tears: her cheeks, her neck, Pancho's cheeks, Pancho's handkerchief, Pancho's shirt collar, the weeds, the tosca soil of the grass lot, the sleeves of Fanny's dress, Fanny's pillow.

Flowers prematurely withered the night of Sunday, April 26, 1937, due to a sudden fall in temperature: the white lily and the white musk roses in Doctor Nastini's garden, and some wild flowers in the gutters of Vallejos's outskirts.

Nocturnal insects not affected: the cockroaches of the construction site, the spiders of the webs woven between unplastered bricks and the beetles flying around the light bulb located in the middle of the street and belonging to the municipal lighting system.

Dr. Juan José Malbrán
Vallejos, Prov. of B.A.
August 23, 1937

Dr. Mario Eugenio Bonifaci
San Roque Hostel
Cosquín, Prov. of Córdoba

Respected Colleague:

First of all let me apologize for my delay in answering your letter, due, believe me, to my wish to become better informed on the Etchepare case. I must confess that I do not understand the boy's reaction. I've known him since he was born and I've always considered him strong-minded, stubborn yes, but always for his own good. So I don't understand why he's not obeying treatment. Neither can I figure out his hurry to get back. I don't exclude the possibility that some pretty girl's at the bottom of it. I do recall a curious detail in that respect: I learned of the seriousness of Etchepare's condition owing to an anonymous letter sent obviously by a woman, which in printed letters that betrayed a feminine hand said Juan Carlos did not want to come to my office so that no one would learn that he was in bad shape, that in her presence he had spit blood, and that I should get Juan Carlos away from his loved ones, something which they didn't have the heart to express. What is noteworthy about this anonymous letter is that it furnished a curious piece of information, it said that Etchepare felt really bad between one and three in the morning.

In any case I think that you people have little left to do now since according to the conversation I had with his mother yesterday, they won't be able to pay the sanatorium expenses beyond the middle of September. I leave it up to your judgment to communicate this news to Etchepare now or further along. For your information his mother is a widow and has almost no money, only enough to get by discreetly. He himself has no savings and his leave from work is without privilege of salary. The mother told me besides that the boy never gave her a cent of his earnings for the house, so I doubt he is so eager to leave Cosquín to save his mother money. He seems indifferent on that point. Really I do not understand why he doesn't take advantage of treatment.

As always at your disposition.

Cordially,
Juan José Malbrán
General Practitioner

Young composer:	(walking along the shores of an Andean lake) It is strange that this unbridled nature does not enthrall you, why your soul is the very reflection of its beauty.
Glamorous widow:	(new in this place) What do you know of my soul?
Young composer:	I think I'm beginning to know it.
Glamorous widow:	In order to know a soul you must first dominate it.

(from the Argentine film *Swan Song*)

Cosquín, Saturday, July 3, 1937

My Darling:

As you see I've kept my promise, of course a little more and my time would have been up, tomorrow the week is over already. How are you? I'll bet you don't even remember who the undersigned is, when we said good-by it looked like you were going to need a whole bed sheet to dry all your tears and dripings, and now tonight if I'm not careful you'll be out on the town already, having a blast. When you come right down to it you didn't cry that much, just a few crocodile tears, which don't come too hard for a woman.

Sweetie pie, what are you doing right this minute? I wish I knew, are you taking a siesta? all snugled up? if only I was a pillow so I could be closer. And not a hot water bag because you might have dirty feet and I'd be done for. Yes, it's better not to be looking for strange things and to be a pilow instead, and if you confide in me who knows what I might find out, an old jipsy told me not to trust blondes, so what are you going to confide to the pilow? if you ask it who loves you it's going to say I do, those pilows are full of bull you know. . . . Well, honey, I'm going to leave you a moment because they're ringing the bell for tea, it's a good idea since this way I can rest a little because I've been writing letters since I finished lunch.

Well, here I am again, you should see how well they treet me, I had two cups of tea with three diferent pastries, with your sweet tooth you'd be right in your element here. Hey, tomorrow's Sunday, are you going to the movies? and who's going to buy you chocolate bars, eh?

Now I'm going to tell you what this place is like, Blondie, like I promised. Look, it's all yours if you want it. It's very nice but I'm bored stif. The hostel is white with a roof of red tiles, like almost all the houses in Cosquín. The town is small, and when one of these skiny marinks couffs at night you can hear him a mile away it's so quiet. There's a river here too, it comes down from the springs in the mountain, you should see the other day when I rented a chaise I went as far as La Falda, where the water is cold and there are trees all around, but by the time it gets to Cosquín it's warm, because here everything's dry and nothing grows, no weeds, no plants, to keep back the sun. I've put this same little paragraf in every letter because if not I'll get cramps in my brains from thinking so much.

And what else? They say that next week when July vacasion begins a lot of tourists come, but it seems that none of them stay to sleep in town, for fear of contagiun, and there's nobody more stinking rotten than them, pardon the expresion. Look, this is going to be over soon, because it's a lot of money being spent for precotion only, what's with all this precotion, if everybody in Vallejos had x-rays taken the place would be empty, and they'd all be here. Well, anything for the old lady, so her baby will get good and well. And you, Blondie, just take care because I left my sentinels posted back there, no dirty triks because I'll find out, you don't think so? Even if it's just rapping a package with one too many frills for some gerk, I'll know about it in no time. Really, I can't forgive a dirty turn, don't you ever forget it.

Doll, I'm running out of paper, I won't tell you any more about life here, you can imagine it: eating and sleeping.

As far as the nurses are concerned, they're all bullet-proof, the youngest went to school with Columbus.

Kisses till you say stop,

Juan Carlos

P.S. Write back immediately like you promised, I'm more bored than you think. At least three pages like I'm sending you.

In the sun on the terrace he gathers his rough drafts, pushes the blanket aside, leaves the lounging chair, and asks a young nurse the room number of the old man he sat opposite during tea in the winter dining room. The door of room fourteen opens and the elderly classics professor invites his visitor to come in. He shows him pictures of his wife, children, and grandchildren. Next he alludes to his eight-year stay at the hostel, the stationary nature of his illness, and the fact that he has never seen any of his three grandchildren for various reasons, principally financial ones. Lastly he takes the rough drafts from the visitor and, as he had promised, corrects the spelling in the three letters: the first—seven pages long —addressed to a young lady, the second—three pages long—addressed to his family, and the third—also three pages long—addressed to another young lady.

*

Cosquín, Saturday, July 27, 1937

My Darling:

Your letter's here right in front of me, how I waited for it, it's dated Thursday, July 8, but the stamp from the Vallejos post ofice says the 10th, why did it take you so long to put it in the mailbox? As you see I've got my gun cocked.

First I recieved a letter from my sister, you should see what a louzy letter, one page and a half that she wrote in class while her pupils did a drawing, you think they drew her short legs? I'm sore at her. The old lady said she'd write me without fail but now she backed out, because her hand is all shaky and she's ashamed to send me scribles. But it's my old lady's handwriting, what do I care if it's scribled. My sister critisizes her so she feels intimedated.

The thing is that in almost twenty days I only recieved that letter and now yours. And now let me uncock my gun and put it on the table, because I want to have my hands free, in this moment I am rubing your little neck with my fingertips, and if you let me I'll undo the little button on the back of your blous, and run my hand down your back, and scratch that soft little hide you have. What a nice letter you sent me . . . is all that you say true?

Here it's business as usual, I'm not giving you details about what we do all day because I don't like to talk about it. You should see the things one sees in this sanatorium, this hostel stuff is pure bull. People even die here, I refused to beleive it, but the other day a seventeen-year-old chick who wasn't coming to the dining room lately died in her room. And I have to put up with this, here I'm really going to get sick, from getting so worked up about things in this place. If

I let them control my whole life I'm finished, because they don't give you free rain in anything, because there are so many doctors that they all get confused in the noodle and don't remember if you're in critical condition or not, and in the end they give everybody the same treatment so they won't make mistakes, they treat you as if tomorrow you were going to kick the bucket. That's why I'm always one step ahead, and I won't tell you everything I do, which in the end isn't much. It so happens that the water in the river is nice and warm, and during siesta it's better than ever, but the regulation is that you have to sleep during siesta or as a special treat lie in the lounging chair on the winter terrace, with a Cordoban blanket that's three times heavier than normal, in the hot sun. Well, little ol' me heels it and takes a swim in the river. I swim in the raw, because I didn't bring my trunks, and since I can't bring a towel I just dry in the sun. If I stepped out of the hostel with a towel in my hand the doorman would smell a rat right away. But the mountain sun is trimendous, and if there's no wind you dry without shivering, I shake the water off like dogs do, and that's it. How can that hurt me? If I take a siesta it's worse, because at night I twist and turn and can't sleep, and the thoughts that come to my mind, well, better left unsaid.

These are things that I'd only tell you, my old lady I don't tell a thing, but I can't stand this place any longer, nobody gets cured here. When you talk to them, nobody tells you when he's thinking of going home, all they think about is the cost, because the hostel is the most expencive place in Cosquín. They're always talking about moving to a private bordinghouse and having an outside doctor treat them, or renting a little house and bringing the family. There's a regular hospital in Cosquín too, and the other day a strange idea got into my ol' gourd and I went to see it, I don't know why, the things one does around here out of pure boredom, you can't imagine, light of my life. How I love to call you light of my life, why I don't know, but when I see you again you're going to make me forget all that I saw, because you're something else, so different.

I'm going to tell you about the poor people's hospital, I'm telling you so you'll know how it is, but promise me you'll never bring the subject up again, being so healthy you can't imagine the noise they make with their couff. In the hostel you can hear a little couffing in the dining room, but luckily there are loudspeakers playing records or the radio on while we eat.

The first day I went to the hospital I had gone out to swim in the river. But a cool wind was blowing, so I wandered around, anything not to drop back and take a siesta and before I knew it I was way up on the mountain, with the hospital right in front of me. The patient in the bed next to the door, in the bad ward, didn't have a visitor so we started talking. He told me about himself, and since they walk around with their pajamas on and the bathrobes they give them there, two others came over to talk too. They took me for an intern and I played along with them.

I don't want to go anymore but I do out of pity to talk to this poor devil in the first bed, and you're not going to beleive this but each time I go there's a new one, do you realize what I'm saying? it's not that anybody gets better, darling, when a bed is vacated it's because one of them died, yes, now don't get scared, only the very critical patients go there, that's why they die.

Now you forget all this, it has nothing to do with you, you're healthy, so touff a bullet wouldn't go through you, you're like the little diamond in the hardwear store that's used to cut glass, but diamonds are colorless like a glass without wine, it's better with wine, nice and red then, like a ruby, my darling. Write soon, be good, and don't take so long to put the letter in the mailbox this time.

I miss you.

Love and many kisses,
Your Juan Carlos

P.S. I forgot to tell you that I have a good friend at the hostel, in the next letter I'll tell you about him.

In the sun on the terrace he gathers his rough drafts, pushes the blanket aside, and leaves the lounging chair. He goes to room fourteen. In the corridor he exchanges an almost imperceptible look of complicity with a young nurse. The patient in room fourteen receives him gladly. Immediately he sits down to correct the spelling of the three letters: the first —half a page long—addressed to a young lady, the second—two pages long—addressed to his sister, and the third—six pages long—addressed to another young lady. Then a long conversation unfolds, during the course of which the visitor tells almost the whole story of his life.

*

Cosquín, August 10, 1937

Light of My Life:

The other day your second letter and my sister's second came both together. Of course there was a diference . . . and that's why I read yours about eighty times and my sister's twice and see you later, alligator. You can tell when somebody writes you just to be nice.

But darling, the leest they can do is write, you won't beleive when I tell you that these four letters are the only ones I've gotten since I've been here, what's the matter with people? are they afraid of catching something through the mail? I swear to you they're going to pay for this. How right my old man was, when you're down everybody gives you the cold shoulder. Did I ever tell you about my old man?

Well, my old man and his brother owned some land forty miles from Vallejos that had been my grandfather's. My old man was a certified public accountant, with a univercity degree from Buenos Aires, know what I mean? he wasn't a simple bookkeeper like me. Well, the old man went to school in the capital because my grandfather made him go, because he saw that the old man was a whizz at numbers, and the other brother who was a brute, stayed to graze with the cows. Well, my grandfather died and the old man continude his schooling and the other meanwhile left him in the lerch, he sold the land, kept almost all the money, and disappeared off the face of the earth, until we found out that he has a ranch now near Tandil. He'll get his yet.

My poor old man had to grin and bear it and so he set up shop in Vallejos, I'm not saying he had a bad life, he did get piles of work, and I don't remember hearing him complane, but when he died of a heart attak the old lady started screeming like a madwoman. And I remember that the doorbell rang the morning after his wake, it was about eight in the morning, and the old lady had heard the train from Buenos Aires, which in those days arrived at seven thirty. We were all sitting around not saying anything, and you could hear the locomotive, and the whistles blowing, from the train that was coming from the capital and going on to the pampas. It seems the old lady thought that the old man's brother was coming on that train, how could he if nobody had notifide him? . . . So it happened that a while later the bell rang and the old lady ran to the shed and grabed the shotgun: she was sure it was that bastard and she wanted to kill him.

But it was the men from the funeral parlor who were

coming to close the box. Then it was that the old lady got it
into her head to start screaming and twisting all over the
place, poor old lady, and to saying that the old man's heart
attak was from all the agravation he had in his life on acount
of his theiving brother, and now he left his two children
without the land that would have rightly belonged to them,
she said the old man had been too noble, and should have
protested or brought a lawsuit against that swindler, but now
the ones who had to suffer were his wife and children. Well,
why go on. It's just that at night when I can't sleep this always comes to my mind.

How faraway all that is, isn't it? And you too are faraway, ruby. And now I'm going to explane why I didn't write
right away, why I let several days go by . . . I was thinking
so much about you, and about other things, to think that
only now that I'm faraway do I realize something . . . I want
to write it down but it's as if my hand was cramped, what's
happening to me, Blondie? am I ashamed of telling lies? I
don't know if I felt the same before, maybe I did and didn't
realize it, because now I feel that I love you very much.

If only you could be nearer to me, if I could see you
come off the bus from Córdoba, it seems that you'd cure my
couff just from making me so hapy. And why can't it be? it's
all the fault of the damn dough, because if I had dough to
throw away I'd send you a money order right now so that
you and your mama could come spend some days. Light of
my life, I miss you, before your letter came I was feeling
strange, afraid that I'd really get sick, but now each time I
read your letter I feel confident again. How hapy we're
going to be, ruby, I'm going to drink all the wine you've got
inside, and I'm going to get good and plastered, hapily plastered, anyway afterward you'll let me take a siesta beside
you, with your store uniform on, in front of your old lady,
don't get scared, she can watch us, and the old man, does

anybody step all over his flower beds now that I'm not there?

Well, my love, write one of your sweet letters real soon, send it off right away, don't think about it like I do.

I love you so much,
Juan Carlos

P.S. Again I forgot to tell you that a very nice man, admited here like me, sends his regards. I had the nerve to show him your letters, and he likes them very much, and he's a very educated person, an ex-professor from the Univercity. Now me he says I write like a donkey.

In the sun on the terrace he gathers his rough drafts, pushes his blanket aside, leaves the lounging chair, and goes to room fourteen. He is amiably received and after attending to the correction of the only existing letter, the visitor must withdraw to his room because of an unexpected hot flush accompanied by a strong cough. The occupant of room fourteen ponders the situation of his young friend and the possible inferences of his case.

Questions Which the Occupant of Room Fourteen Formulated Upon Considering His Friend's Predicament

would Juan Carlos dare, if he knew the graveness of his condition, to bind a woman to his life in marriage?

was Juan Carlos conscious of the graveness of his condition?

would Nené agree, if she was a virgin, to marry a consumptive?

would Nené agree, if she wasn't a virgin, to marry a consumptive?

if Juan Carlos did feel something new for Nené and that was the reason why he had decided to propose marriage to her upon his return to Vallejos, why did he so often recall Nené's awkwardness that day long ago when she served him an overflowing glass of homemade liqueur on a breakfast saucer?

why did he constantly repeat that Mabel was selfish and bad but that she knew how to dress and serve tea in an impeccable fashion?

EIGHTH EPISODE

> Your song bears the chill of the last
> rendezvous.
>
> (from H. Manzi's tango "Malena")

Cosquín, August 19, 1937

Dearest Darling:

I recieved your letter at noon, just before going into the dining room, and already I'm answering you. Today I'm not ashamed of anything. I'm going to tell you everything I feel, I'm so hapy I could jump off this terrace to the garden below, I've been feeling like doing that for a long time, it's very high, but today I'm sure that I would fall firmly on my feet and skamper off like a cat with my bones in one piece.

You will say that I'm naughty but one thing I liked about your letter is that the manager scolded you because you go to the bathroom so much, to hide when you feel like crying for me. Sily little thing, you shouldn't cry, but do you really love me that much?

Today I'm making a promise, which is that I'm going to follow all the doctors' directions, the other day they scolded me, and since we have to be seperated anyway, let it be for a good cause, so that when you see me set foot in Vallejos it'll be because I'm totally cured and don't have to come back here again, it's not really such an awfull place, but it's far from you and that's awfull. Now you have to promise me one thing: that you're not going to go around crying on the sly, even if I have to stay here until New Year's, and be assured that when I leave this place it's because I'm healthy. It's a bit expensive but one's health is priceless. And when I'm back in Vallejos we'll start a new life, together forever, do you accept? Then start making plans.

The truth is I was clowning around with the treatment, but from now on everything's going to change, the hardest part is going to be staying away from the river, the doctor found out about my swimming and just about kicked me out of his office. But I feel so hapy now, how funny, I remember the day my old man gave me permition to take a bike ride to the field that had been grandfather's. I had heard him mention it so many times that I wanted to see what it was like, I was about nine or ten at the time, and when I got there I saw another kid near the main house which they had built just recently. The kid was riding around on a little colt, only because they didn't let him play with the ranch hands, he was the owner's son and he started playing with me, and he asked me for half the veel cutlets my old lady had prepared for me. And when they called him in for lunch, the nursemaid realized that he was already eating and she made me come inside the house so that I could finish filling myself. They must have seen that I wasn't any old tramp and they sat me down at the table, first they took me to wash my hands, and his mother

In the sun on the terrace he stops writing, pushes his blanket aside, leaves the lounging chair, and goes to room fourteen. He is cordially received. As usual he hands over the rough draft but this time interjects a variant: besides spelling corrections he asks for help in wording the letter at issue. His plan is to send a well-written love letter, and this request is received enthusiastically. The professor immediately proposes a letter in which he compares the girl in question to the Lethe, and he explains in detail that this is a mythological river situated at the exit from Purgatory where the purified souls bathe to wash away bad memories before undertaking the flight to Paradise. The young man laughs sardonically and rejects the proposal for being "a lot of bull." His interlocutor is offended and adds that a sick man should distrust women's promises, if they offer a great deal there is the possibility that they are moved by pity rather than love. The young man lowers his eyes and asks permission to retire to rest in his room while the revision of the letter is carried out. At the door he raises his head and looks the old man in the eyes. The latter takes this opportunity to add that it is unfair to submit a girl to such a destiny. Once in bed the young man tries to take an afternoon nap as prescribed by the doctors. His nerves only allow him a partial repose, since his sleep is disturbed by frequent nightmares.

Images and words that passed through Juan Carlos's mind as he slept: a brick oven, human bones with ribs and dripping fat, a roasting spit in the middle of the fields, a side of ribs roasting over a slow fire, peasants looking for coal and dry branches to feed the fire, a peasant in charge of watching the roast drinks a whole bottle of wine and falls asleep letting the roast burn, the meat dries, the wind flares up the burning coals and the flames sputter sparks, a dead man is pierced by the spit and exposed to the fire, a vertical iron shaft nailed to the ground pierces his heart, another shaft pierces his ribs and holds his arms open, the dead man moves and moans, he is reduced to bones partially covered by dry and scorched hide, human bones stained with black fat, a long dark corridor, a windowless cell, a woman's hands bring a wet rag and soap, a cup full of warm water, her back turned a woman goes to the river to bring more water in the cup, Nené rubs the rag between her hands and a very white lather gushes out, she washes carefully the bones fallen among the ashes of the spit, "think, Juan Carlos, what a beautiful idea this river Lethe is where one leaves bad memories behind, those souls approach with unsure step, everything reminds them of passed torments, they see pain where there is none because they carry it inside themselves, and as they pass they spill it out, staining everything," a syringe with a thick needle sinks between the ribs of a broad virile chest, the patient doesn't suffer on account of the anesthesia and thanks nurse Nené, suddenly the young man cries out with pain because another hand is applying an injection to his neck, Nené pulls crust off the bones and somebody thanks her, Doctor Nastini corners Nené in the corridor of the hospital and pulls up her skirt by force, a longer corridor is dark and there are bones all over the floor, Nené looks for a broom and sweeps them carefully so that it won't hurt the bones, Nené is the only living person, "the souls come out of those black expiatory caverns and bright angels point to a river of clear waters, the souls draw near, fearful," the bones are hollow and weigh nothing, a wind rises and carries them upward, bones fly in the air, the wind carries them away with dirt and leaves and other garbage, "the souls finally anoint themselves in the waters, blinded by a veil of sorrows that hid everything from them, now they raise their eyes and see for the first time the face of · heaven, Juan Carlos, pull off your veil of sorrows, it can hide the clearest heavens from your eyes," smoke is coming from burning garbage, the strong wind raises the garbage in whirlwinds and carries it far away, the wind tears roofs off houses and tumbles trees from their roots, tin roof sheets fly in the air, there are fallen bones among the weeds, a stagnant pond, the water is foul, someone asks Nené for a glass of water, Nené doesn't hear because she's far away, someone asks Nené to please bring a glass of water because the thirst is unbearable, Nené doesn't hear, someone asks Nené to change the pillowcase, Nené looks at the bloodstains on the pillow, someone asks Nené if that nauseates her, a patient assures Nené that he wasn't coughing and that the pillowcase is splattered with red ink, Nené refuses to believe him, someone tells Nené that it's red ink or tomato sauce but not blood, a woman stifles her laugh but it's not Nené, that hidden woman is laughing at Nené's nurse apron with big bloodstains, someone asks Nené if when she worked as a nurse was it blood or red ink or tomato sauce that dirtied her apron, Nené brings a glass of water to the thirsty patient, the thirsty patient promises not to swim anymore in the river, the patient promises his mother to shave before going to work and to eat all the food they serve him, the train from Buenos Aires arrives on a cold morning at the Vallejos station, the train arrives but it is night, Juan Carlos is dead in the coffin, Juan Carlos's mother hears the whistle of the locomotive and exchanges a look with Celina, Juan Carlos tells his mother that he choked on his own blood while coughing and that's why the pillow in the coffin in which he lies is stained with blood, his mother and sister go to the shed, choking on blood, Juan Carlos tries to shout to them not to kill his uncle, not to look for the shotgun, the uncle knocks on the door, Juan Carlos tries to warn him of the danger he's in, the uncle comes in and Juan Carlos notices that he looks a lot like the occupant of room fourteen, Juan Carlos assures his uncle that he has mended his ways and shaves in the morning, and that he's a hard worker, the uncle has some documents in his hand and Juan Carlos entertains the hope that they are the papers which will make him owner of his uncle's ranch, Juan Carlos hides what he's thinking from the uncle and offers himself as manager instead, the uncle doesn't answer but smiles kindly and retires to rest in room fourteen, Juan Carlos thinks that when the uncle wakes up he's going to tell his relative that his mother and sister have always spoken badly of him, the uncle returns inopportunely and Juan Carlos reproaches him for lodging in room fourteen instead of remaining on his ranch, Juan Carlos hears footsteps, his mother and sister are approaching with the rifle, in vain Juan Carlos tries to warn his uncle of the danger he's in, Juan Carlos is dead in the box and cannot do anything, the barrel of the gun is thick and the head of the occupant of room fourteen breaks into pieces like an eggshell, the stains are of blood, Juan Carlos thinks that he won't need to lie to anybody and he will tell everyone they are bloodstains and not red ink or tomato sauce.

*

Cosquín, August 31, 1937

Light of My Life:

I was waiting for your letter today but it never came. I'm writing to you just the same because I got a letter from home and things are in a bit of a mess. It looks like I have to go back to Vallejos and then come back here to complete the cure, as soon as possible. The old lady wants me personally to take charge of dealing with the tenents in the two houses to try to raize the rent.

You know something? the doctor told me I'm doing better, now I do everything he says.

A loving kiss,
Juan Carlos

Without having written a rough draft he takes the written page, puts it in an envelope, and hurries to give it to the doorman before the mail pickup at 4:00 P. M. The temperature is high for the time of year, there isn't any wind blowing. He thinks of the

warm water of the river. He goes to room fourteen
to suggest a game of cards to pass the time until tea.

*

Cosquín, September 9, 1937

Light of My Life:

I may arrive before these lines do but all the same I feel
like talking to you a bit. I'm not well, in spirit I mean.

Now I'm going to ask you a favor, and this is for real,
please don't tell anybody, not even your family, that I'm
coming back without completing the cure. Until the last minute I was hoping that my sister and the old lady would fix
things so I wouldn't have to come, but not a chance. The
people at my ofice don't want to extend my leeve, what's it
to them, it's without salary anyway.

I'm thinking that if I fix everything I'll be back here as
soon as possible. Imagine, Blondie, just from talking to you a
little I feel better, how will it be when I see you! Today was
one of the worst days of my life.

Be seeing you soon.

Love and kisses,
Juan Carlos

In the sun on the terrace he gathers his rough drafts,
pushes the blanket aside, leaves the lounging chair,
and looks around, searching for something new to
divert his eyes. He doesn't find anything. He thinks
of the fact that the young nurse Matilde will be on
duty that night, ready to rush to her patients' calls.
He desperately wants a cigarette. He looks at the
sky. There are no clouds and the wind isn't blowing. Despite the fact that teatime is near he decides
to take a swim in the river, besides it will be one of

his last chances to swim, since his departure is set for three days hence.

DEPARTMENT OF PUBLIC HEALTH
FOR THE PROVINCE OF BUENOS AIRES

REGIONAL HOSPITAL FOR THE DISTRICT OF VALLEJOS

Date: June 11, 1937.
Ward: General Clinic.
Physician: Dr. Juan José Malbrán.
Patient: Antonia Josefa Ramírez.
Diagnosis: Normal Pregnancy.
Symptoms: Last menstruation second week in April, vomiting, nausea, general state of patient confirmative.
Notes: Expected date of confinement in maternity ward last week in January. Patient residing at 488 Alberti Street, as maidservant of Mr. Antonio Sáenz, single, did not reveal name presumed father. *Pass duplicate file to maternity ward.*

*

POLICE DEPARTMENT OF THE PROVINCE OF BUENOS AIRES

Police Station or Division: Vallejos.
Records Sent to: Local Files.
Date: July 29, 1937.
Text: It is hereby acknowledged that on the above date, at 7:15 P.M., the following applicants for the position of police officer will embark on the passenger train bound for the federal capital: Narciso Angel Bermúdez, Francisco Catalino Páez, and Federico Cuello. They will be accompanied by First Sergeant Romualdo Castanos, carrier of the required documentation such as the enrollment card and registration docket of each of the applicants. First Sergeant Castaños will accompany them as far as the transfer from Independence Station of the Western Railroad to Constitution Square Station of the Southern Railroad where they will embark on the first

available train bound for the city of La Plata, where they will report immediately to Division No. 2 of the Province Police Department. The courses are expected to be initiated on the first day of August for a duration of six months.

Benito Jaime García
Lieutenant in Charge

*

DEPARTMENT OF AGRICULTURE AND LIVESTOCK
FOR THE PROVINCE OF BUENOS AIRES

La Plata, September 12, 1937

ADMINISTRATIVE ORDER
PRESENTATION OF CLAIM—Copy for files

On this date at desk three the deed of sale and record of proceedings raised before the police captain of Vallejos by arraignment of Mr. Cecil Brough-Croydon, resident of the Percival Ranch in the District of Vallejos, were presented against Mr. Antonio Sáenz, auctioneer, residing at Alberti No. 488, Vallejos, the latter accused of having sold the former cattle with chronic defects, such as ticks and carbuncle.

*

. . . the bus, the jolt, the dust cloud, the window, the fields, the wire fence, the cows, the pasture, the driver, the cap, the window, the horse, a shack, the telegraph pole, the telephone pole, the back of the seat in front, the legs, the trouser crease, the jolt, the backsides, no smoking in this vehicle, the chewing gum, the window, the fields, the cows, the pasture, the corn, the alfalfa, a chaise, a farm, a grocery store, a house, the Gaucho Inn General Store, a field of sunflowers, Social Club-Sports Headquarters, the shacks, the houses, the window, the lampposts, the dirt road, the asphalt, Public Auctioneer Antonio P. Sáenz, doctor's office-Doctor Nastini, the pavement, the lights, the Argentine Bargain Store, Bank of the Province, the Western Arrow Bus Company, the brakes, the legs, the cramps, the hat, the poncho, the suitcase, my sister, the hug, the cheeks, the wind, the poncho, the cold, the cough, three blocks, the suitcase, the Argentine Bargain Store, doctor's office-Doctor Nastini, the League bar, the sweat, the armpits, the feet, the groin, the itching, the neighbors, the sidewalk, the opened front door, my mother, the black shawl, the hug, the tears, the entranceway, the foyer, the suitcase, the dust, the poncho, the cough, the suntan, eleven pounds heavier, Cosquín, the mayor's office, the rent hikes, the leave, the hostel, the budget, the doctor, the diagnosis, the treatment, the x-ray, the room, the bed, the night table, the kerosene heater, the wardrobe, the bathroom, the warm water, the bathtub, the washstand, the toilet, the hook, the towel, the heater, the mirror, the consumptive, the athlete, the sexual organ, the suntan, the sweat, the itching, the cramps, the faucet, the gush of warm water, the soap, the lather, the perfume, Nené, Nurse Matilde, Nené, Mabel, Nené, Nené, Nené, engagement ring, the lukewarm water, the wooden mat, the slippers, the drops of water, the towel, the heater, the flames, the chills, the underwear, the razor, the soap, the beard, the cologne, the comb, the cowlick, the table, my mother, my sister, the dishes, the napkin, the news in Vallejos, carbuncle, carbuncle, the scandal, Mabel, the Englishman, the accusation, bankruptcy, Mabel, the soup, the spoon, the noodles, carbuncle, the swindle, the bread, a spoonful of meat extract in the soup, the broken engagement, the ranch, the ranches, the wine, the soda water, the water, steak with mashed potatoes, the bread, the wine, my mother, the leave, the salary, the budget, the picnic, Mabel, the moans, the tears, the knife, the fork, the steak, the mashed potatoes, the wine, bankruptcy, the teaching job, the swindle, the shame, my little piece of ass, the picnic, the embrace, the kiss, the pain, the blood. the grass, the cheeks, the lips, the tears on her mouth, the Englishman, the arraignment, the

swindle, bankruptcy, the disgrace, poverty, the mashed potatoes, the baked apple, the syrup, my mother, my sister, the
coffee cup, a quarter after nine, the night, the cold, the poncho, the sidewalk, the wind, the dirt streets, the corner, the
gate, the hedge, the blonde, Nené, my girlfriend, the mother,
the father, the kitchen, the table, the oilcloth, Cosquín, the
treatment, the final cure, the mayor's office, my job, the
plans, the intentions, her father the gardener, the sidewalk,
the gate, Nené, the father, the flowerbed, the hedge, the dirt
sidewalk, the house without whitewash, the packing job, the
white skin, the lips, the cold, the wind, the gate, the light in
the kitchen, the mother in the kitchen, women's promises,
"you're not completely cured? but there's little to go, I'm
sure by New Year's you'll be completely cured, was the bus
trip very tiring?" room fourteen, the old man, would you
marry a sick man? "it doesn't matter one bit, but don't do
that please . . . take your hand away, Juan Carlos," Doctor
Nastini, my sister, the gossip, "it's better to wait for the wedding night, that way we'll be good a few months more and
you'll be cured once and for all, and listen I'm afraid they
might see us at this gate, and you're sure you'll still love me
afterward? let's wait a bit more till they fall asleep, but remember, Juan Carlos, it's because you asked me to," will I be
fired from the mayor's office? will they fire her from school?
just two in a shack, cheeseparing and candle ends, no, unless
you ask me I won't even touch your hands, you ask me,
Nené, show me that you truly love me, that nothing matters,
"no dear, if I ask you for that you'll say I'm cheap, never
that, and papa and mama might come out, and I'm afraid,
Juan Carlos, why are men that way? aren't you happy with
holding me in your arms?" the gate, the hedge, the wind, the
cold, "Juan Carlos, don't go away mad!" the corner, the
paved streets, the lampposts, the sidewalks, the houses, the
closed windows, the closed doors, the corners, the dark, the

construction site, the new police station, the finished entrance, the lock, the chain, Mabel, Mabel, Mabel! I want to see you, tomorrow, in daylight, I'm going to tell you that I came back . . . because I'm cured! and that I don't care if you're bankrupt, doesn't every cloud have a silver lining? what luck that I came back! the lamppost, the sidewalk, the asphalt, the wind, the cold, the dark, the construction site, the finished entrance, the lock, the chain, every cloud has a silver lining

A tango lingers on blue, violet, black lips

NINTH EPISODE

I will always blame that tango
and the wooer with his wiles,
once he'd made my heart break
all he told me was good-by.

(from Roldan's "Blame That Tango")

RECAPITULATION: Upon his return from Cosquín, Juan Carlos Etchepare tried to see María Mabel Sáenz, in vain, since the young woman had gone away, although not without first obtaining the school board's permission. The leave was immediately granted her, with salary. Her parents saw her off at the railroad station and remained on the platform until the train was out of sight, bound for Buenos Aires. Shortly thereafter, conversations between Dr. Malbrán and the mayor decided the fate of Juan Carlos: the young man was not in condition to return to work and neither could they extend his leave. Without further ado he was dismissed and this circumstance had an immediate repercussion in the home of Nélida Enriqueta Fernández, where among others, the following charges were heard: "As Nené's father I have the right to ask you those questions!" "If you cannot return to work it's because you're not well!" "How dare you come near my daughter if you're not healthy?" "Don't you have any conscience? what if she catches it?" Juan Carlos took offense, convinced that a gardener wasn't in any position to scold him. But the days spent in the bar grew long and not daring to confide his troubles in anyone, he missed Pancho. Juan Carlos wished his friend would drop the course being given in the capital of the province so that he could come back and keep him company, and talking to the police captain during a poker game, he inadvertently alluded to the Sáenz maid's pregnancy.

January 27, 1938

Taking a break in the day's activity, at 12:48 Nélida Enriqueta Fernández wiped her mouth with her napkin, folded it, and left the table with the purpose of taking an hour's siesta. In her room she took off her shoes and the blue cotton uniform. She pulled back the bedspread and lay down on the sheet. The temperature was 102.2 in the shade, a high point for that summer. She looked for a comfortable position, on her side. The pillow bothered her and she pushed it to one side. She turned face down. In spite of having taken off the shoes her feet still hurt, with sores and raw spots between the toes, caused by acidic sweat; under the big toe of her right foot the burning sensation from a budding blister was starting to let up. With one hand she rearranged the hairpins to free her neck of the heat accumulated in her hair, sweeping it upward. Her neck was damp from an almost imperceptible layer of perspiration, from her scalp a round drop of sweat dripped down, and then another. The straps of her brassiere and petticoat, also damp, dug into her skin, she moved them down below her shoulder. She had to bring her arms together against her body so as not to strain the seams. The drops bursting out of her armpits expanded, new ones burst out. She returned the straps to their place and turned face up with her arms spread out away from her body. She had shaved her armpits and the skin there was reddened by the application of antiperspirants. Her back, in contact with the bed, heated the sheets and the mattress. She moved toward the edge of the bed looking for a cooler strip of sheet and mattress. An uncomfortable itch, of sweaty skin, began to bother her. Breathing was difficult, the air pushed her diaphragm slowly and forcefully downward. Her tense throat registered nervous spasms and saliva passed down with difficulty. The pressure of her skull upon her temples increased, possibly due to the one and a half glasses of wine with lemon and ice taken during lunch. Around her eyes an internal tremor inflamed her eyelids, she felt that a load of tears was about to burst over her face. Something weighed more and more upon her, like a stone, in the center of her chest.

What in that moment was her greatest desire?

In that moment her greatest desire was that Juan Carlos get his job back at the mayor's office.

What in that moment was her greatest fear?

In that moment her greatest fear was that someone would make a point of telling the young public auctioneer just arrived in Vallejos—with whom she had danced so much at the Christmas gala—about her past dubious relationship with Dr. Nastini.

On the aforementioned January 27, 1938, taking a break in the day's activity, at 9:30 P.M., Juan Carlos Etchepare prepared to smoke his one cigarette for the day, sitting in the garden. Before sunset his mother had watered the planters and the gravel paths, and the wet soil gave off a cool air along with its invigorating smell. The lighter produced a small flame, the cigarette lit up and released hot white smoke. The darker smoke which Juan Carlos exhaled formed a transparent mountain, behind it were the planters of palm trees surrounded by hyacinth hedges, four planters, four palm trees, further back the chicken coop and the garden wall, past the wall the eucalyptus trees in a yard of scrap iron, but beyond that there were no mountains to be seen. The flat pampas, wind and dust, behind the cloud óf dust he had barely managed to see her from afar, she got into the car with her father and mother, the car took off raising another whirlwind of dust. The cigarette was reduced to a butt, he threw it into a planter. His right hand automatically groped for the packet in his shirt pocket. Should he smoke another? Teachers' salaries varied between 125 and 200 pesos, leave with salary was difficult to get if the mayor, Mr. Sáenz's friend, didn't intervene. Two hundred and fifty pesos per month would be enough to pay for the hostel and cover small personal expenses. Not even a regular leave without salary? Employee Etchepare's discharge was signed by the mayor, and the secretary and treasurer of the municipal government; the hot smoke of the second cigarette filled his chest with a pleasant sensation.

What in that moment was his greatest desire?

In that moment his greatest desire was somehow to get hold of the money to leave town and continue the cure in Cosquín's most expensive sanatorium.

What in that moment was his greatest fear?

In that moment his greatest fear was dying.

On the aforementioned January 27, 1938, taking a break in the day's activity, at 5:30 P.M., back from the beauty parlor where she had submitted herself to a wearisome permanent wave, María Mabel Sáenz asked her aunt for the morning newspaper and retired to her room to rest. She took off her street clothes and put on a fresh housecoat. She placed the electric fan on the night table and closed the shutters halfway, letting through the necessary light to read the movie listings in the newspaper. Nothing could be better than choosing an air-conditioned theater where she and her aunt, also a movie fan, could escape from the stifling heat of the city of Buenos Aires. The only sacrifice was taking the sweltering subway, which in ten minutes would deposit them in the middle of downtown Buenos Aires, where the principal air-conditioned movie theaters were located. She looked for the special section, opening the newspaper to the first page. The movies were not on the second page, nor on the third, nor on the fourth, fifth, sixth, seventh, eighth. She felt an increasing nervous irritation, she decided to leaf through the newspaper back to front but on the last page and the one before last there were only real estate ads, the same on the preceding, and on the next, and the next. Her irritation reached its peak, she crushed the newspaper into a ball and threw it against the fan. She attributed her nerves to the long hours spent in the beauty parlor under the dryer. She weeped tearlessly, sank her face into the pillow, and reflected. Why was she so nervous, beauty parlor or no beauty parlor? She blamed the long days of idleness and the nights of insomnia, lying inert in her bed. When she regained her calm she smoothed the sheets of the newspaper and renewed her search for the page in question. There was air conditioning in the Opera theater: *The Lancer Spy* with George Sanders and Dolores del Río; air conditioning also in the Gran Rex: *Stage Door* with two of her favorites, Katharine Hepburn and Ginger Rogers, but being a premiere would there be seats?; in the Monumental: *Three Argentines in Paris* with Florencio Parravicini, Irma Córdoba, and Hugo del Carril; she only went to Argentine movies in Vallejos when there was nothing else to do; in the Gran Cine Florida a European program, *The Secret of the Pompadour* with Kathe von Nagy and Willy Eicherberg, German, and *The Chaste Susana* with Henri Garat and Meg Lemonnier; another double feature in the Rose Marie: *Saratoga* with Jean Harlow, "the platinum blonde in all her posthumous glory," and *You Can't Have Everything* with Alice Faye, Don Ameche, and the Ritz Brothers. Which was the theater that according to her aunt would attract the most distinguished audience? The Ambassador: "air conditioning, Metro-Goldwyn-Mayer presents an exquisite comedy of romantic intrigue with Luise Rainer, William Powell, and Maureen O'Sullivan, *The Emperor's Candlesticks*. Wasn't there any first run with Robert Taylor? No.

What in that moment was her greatest desire?

In that moment her greatest desire was to see Robert Taylor secretly enter her room, or in his place Tyrone Power, with a bunch of red roses in his hand and a voluptuous design in his eyes.

What in that moment was her greatest fear?

In that moment her greatest fear was that her father would lose the lawsuit filed by her detested ex-fiancé Cecil, which would bring significant damage upon the financial and social position of the Sáenz family.

On the aforementioned January 27, 1938, taking a break in the day's activity, at 5:45 P.M., Francisco Catalino Paez dropped onto the hard bed at the barracks. Target practice was over for the day, again he had performed outstandingly, as in the theory classes which had taken place in the morning. The thick Sanforized material of his work shirt was stuck to his sweat-soaked body. He decided to give himself a treat after the bath and went into the shower room adjoining his quarters. The water came out cold but not as cold as the water from the pump behind the shack. And he didn't have to pump, the water came out by itself, generously, just by turning a faucet, he could waste it. They had furlough that evening, but he couldn't miss dinner in the barracks or spend money on a trolley car, and downtown La Plata was far away. Just the same he took his brand-new officer's uniform out of the closet and passed his fingertips along the gabardine of the jacket and trousers, along the shiny leather of the boots, along the golden threads of the epaulets, along the metal buttons, all identical, without manufacturing defects, polished, sewn to the gabardine with double thread. He dressed slowly, fearful of tearing some seam, or of scratching the surface of the boots. He was alone in the barracks, they had all gone. He went to the lavatory and observed at length the officer in the mirror. The removal of his long mustache plus the crewcut changed his features, revealing an almost adolescent appearance. However, with the cap on, the strength of his eyes was accentuated, they were man's eyes, with a wrinkle or two: he used to squint when receiving the frozen gush of water from the pump, and when juggling the bricks passed from hand to hand as the bricklayers unloaded a truck, and when forcing the pick or shovel into the rock soil with all his strength, and when noticing in an occasional mirror on the street that his hand-me-down trousers, besides being worn, were big or small on him. He took off the cap with the shiny eyeshade, put it on again, trying it slightly tilted to one side.

What in that moment was his greatest desire?

In that moment his greatest desire was to stroll down the main streets of Vallejos, with his brand-new uniform on.

What in that moment was his greatest fear?

In that moment his greatest fear was that Fanny would denounce him at the Vallejos Police Station as the father of the forthcoming child.

On the aforementioned January 27, 1938, taking a break in the day's activity, Antonia Josefa Ramírez, at 11:30 P.M., was resting on a stretcher in the maternity ward of the Regional Hospital of Vallejos. She had been moved there in an emergency one hour before, after walking four blocks from her shack with acute pains to the first house with a telephone. Her aunt was working as usual as a maid in a house in the center of town and would not be back until late. The nurse considered it a false alarm, but she would wait for the doctor to return from the emergency room to examine the patient, before deciding whether to admit her or send her home. The nurse went and came, leaving the door open. Fanny sat up and saw men in the dimly lit courtyard, probably husbands of the girls inside, and also old women with white hair, probably mothers or mothers-in-law, waiting for the news to come any minute. Pancho was far away, but it was for everybody's good: he was becoming an officer, when he came back he would make a good living, he had been gone since July 29, she hadn't seen him for almost six months now, and she had kept her promise, not to say anything to anybody. When he was secure in his position they would be able to fix everything, but why hadn't he answered her letters? could they have gotten lost? was her writing so clumsy that the mailman hadn't understood it? One of the boys in the courtyard looked like Pancho, maybe only because of the thick mustache and the long curly hair, he was nervous, he paced the floor smoking. Fanny wanted so much to hold Pancho's big hand, then he would kiss her gently, Fanny would feel his thick mustache brush against her and she would caress his head, his long, curly hair. The light bulb over the courtyard was small and owing to the heat there were more insects than usual flying around it, horse flies, green lacewings, beetles.

What in that moment was her greatest desire?

In that moment her greatest desire was for the baby to be born healthy.

What in that moment was her greatest fear?

In that moment her greatest fear was that Pancho would come back and disown her and the baby.

Dear Mabel,

Just as I promised I'm writing the letter you insisted so much upon, you naughty thing. First of all I hope these lines find you in good health, likewise your family. I think it was in sixth grade when we made this promise, we were only twelve years old, and already all we thought about was boyfriends. Well, I was the first to go on a honeymoon, so it's up to me to begin.

First of all thank you so much for the lovely gift, what a beautiful lamp, the white tulle of the shade is simply exquisite, just the kind I wanted for my wedding gown, but there was no finding it, it must be imported. And besides, needless to say, this gift meant more to me than just that: it meant that deep down we had never stopped being friends. It's not that a girl is materialistic, how shall I say, I mean you had already stopped me on the street to congratulate me with all your heart, and I realized then that we were the same friends as before, but the day before my wedding, when the lamp arrived, I looked at it and called mama to show her that my schoolmate hadn't forgotten me. And what a good choice you made! Again, thanks a million.

Where should I begin? From the church we went back to mama's house, toasted by the few relatives and my inlaws who had come from Trenque Lauquen, and at about nine thirty I had already changed, I put on for the first time the two-piece suit I had spoken to you so much about, and we rode off in the car, which is a piece of junk but it moves. Up until that point I hadn't been emotional, being so nervous what with the long dress, and the suitcases not packed yet, and fighting with mama till the last moment because she insisted that I bring the wedding gown to Buenos Aires to have my picture taken here. Well, in the end I listened to her, but we still haven't had our picture taken, tomorrow morning

I'm going to ask prices at the photograph studios on Callao Street—excuse me, Callao Avenue, Massa gets angry when I mix names up like that—because I saw some good studios there. As I was saying, what with the long ceremony in the church, and in the morning the civil ceremony, the dress and the hairdo, and the tulle headpiece that looked so awful on me when I tried it on, I didn't feel anything, just nervous, and dry in the mouth, dying of thirst, but when I put on the two-piece suit I started to feel funny, and getting into the car and saying good-by to mama I felt so emotional, Mabel, that I started crying like crazy. They came up from my chest, from my very heart, the tears. When he started the car, my husband looked at my face and laughed, but he also felt emotional, because he had seen his mother crying too, poor lady, she seems to be real nice. I lowered my veil and fooled him, I didn't want him to see me with my makeup running. Luckily the dirt road had been flattened by the rain and we reached Lincoln at around midnight. There we spent the night, and after lunch the next day we continued on to Buenos Aires. By about seven o'clock we were already entering Buenos Aires, straight down Rivadavia Avenue, what lights! my husband pointed out the different districts we passed, Ciudadela, Flores, Caballito, what pretty names—no?—Independence Square, right to this lovely hotel, enormous, four stories high, and old but well preserved, it's on Callao Avenue and near to, of all places, Congress.

I had only been to Buenos Aires twice, once when I was little, and the other time when they admitted grandma to the hospital, already critical. We were in mourning and didn't go anywhere. The first thing I did this time was to bring her flowers, although it cost me an argument with Massa, he wants to do everything his own way, but he's very nice, I'm not complaining. Well, what I want to tell you is that I hardly knew the place, really. And the hotel is very steep but it's worth it, it's a good place for my husband because he has to receive businessmen here.

That's why we came to Buenos Aires for our honeymoon, so that he can settle certain matters. Look, maybe it brings bad luck to talk about things before they're done, but I can't keep it back. It so happens that Massa doesn't care a fig for Vallejos. He says he hasn't seen a more gossipy and nauseatingly envious town than Vallejos, according to him Trenque Lauquen is not as progressive but the people are nicer. Now, the place where he wants to live is . . . here. How do you like that! What an ambitious little thing fatso turned out to be. And he has some friends from his town here who are doing well, and that's where we come in. In the meantime we decided to stay a week more, instead of shopping for the house we had planned on. In any case we already have many lovely things with the presents we got, now it's just a matter of setting them up right.

You must be saying that I'm talking a lot, but not about the honeymoon itself. First of all, Mabel, he's a very but really very nice boy. By that I don't mean to say he doesn't have character, but just that he thinks only of our future, and of our having all the modern conveniences, and he's always thinking of what I like so that he can buy it for me to make less work for me in the house. And when he has an afternoon free, because in the morning he always goes out to attend to his things, like I was saying, in the afternoon we go out to look at refrigerators, we've already picked out a Victrola, and if I convince him, one of the first things we're going to buy is an electric fan that I saw, those small ones are the newest thing, all cream colored. And when I think that I don't have to go to the store anymore, I can't believe it, pinch me Mabel, so that I'll know I'm not dreaming.

Of course there's a lot of work waiting for me when I get back to Vallejos, with the wedding so rushed and all, and

I can imagine what they're saying in Vallejos and may their tongues fall out, as I was saying what with the rush and all I didn't even put new curtains in my room. How disgusting people are, the things they'll be saying, that Massa doesn't have a place to hang his hat, that we're going to live in mama's house. They'll soon see, because if they're waiting for new developments before the famous nine months, we'll give them new developments, the move to the capital that's what, and if that fails, well, we already have a cottage in mind, in town, on a paved street. I'm telling you these personal things because you and your family know deep down how mean people can be, from all the months of that ordeal you went through, that's why I tell you things, because you can understand me.

My husband wants to know which I prefer in Buenos Aires, a little apartment downtown or a house with a courtyard in the suburbs. Oh, Mabel, I'm so thrilled that I want to stay downtown. Well, now I'll tell you what I do in the morning. Massa likes breakfast in the room, and while we're at it, that's the moment I have the hardest time getting used to: him catching me in the morning with the mug I have when I wake up, boy does that make me mad! Well, he goes out and I sew the curtains, and look, if the stay in mama's house is just for a short while it doesn't matter, she'll keep them, she needs something to cheer her up a little, you've probably heard that Papa isn't at all well. But let's not talk about sad things. As I was saying, I'm making curtains for the room that was mine when I was single, I found a lovely fabric, and not expensive, so I bought it and I'm doing them. I dress up for lunch and if I manage to keep Massa from taking a siesta, when he's free we go out I told you, and if I'm alone, I visit all the places in the capital that I want to. It's very easy, already I'm learning the names of the streets, I went by myself to the Viceroy Court, the Tower of the English, the skyscraper facing it, the Retiro Station, the port, and I went up on a military ship which allows visitors. Tomorrow I'm going to the Constitution Square Station, and my husband (you know, I'm still not used to saying my husband), well, my husband, has promised to take me to the old Boca Port, I wouldn't go alone because there are a lot of hoodlums there. By seven I'm always waiting for him back at the hotel, because he sometimes comes in with some businessman and we go out for an apéritif. A good thing this week I was smart enough to ask in the hotel if they had rates without dinner, so that we could dine out, and I had my way. It's the only solution, really, because with dinner paid in the hotel where they serve such good food, we were stuffing ourselves like animals, and, afterward, as you can imagine what men are like on honeymoons, he didn't want to go out.

So, Mabel, since Monday when we began to eat out things have changed, because if you have to pay you no longer eat like a pig as in the hotel, you have enough but you don't stuff yourself. So, I always walk him toward the obelisk, as if we were going no place special, and before he knows it Mr. Massa is at the obelisk. There you have restaurants by the dozens, and now do you realize what I'm getting at? We finish eating at just about nine thirty right smack in the theater and movie district, and he can't refuse. Monday the theater companies had their day off and we went to the movies, simply grand, *Algiers* with Charles Boyer and a new girl whose name I don't remember, the most divine woman I've ever seen, and meanwhile I got to see the Opera theater that you had mentioned so often. How right you were, what luxury, it's hard to believe, just as you enter on the sides I saw those palace-type balconies in full array, the imitation plants looked perfect, and the stained-glass windows, and above the screen that rainbow, I was speechless, when my husband nudges me and points to the ceiling . . . I'm almost ready to scream with the stars shining and the clouds moving, why it's like a real sky! The movie was good but just the same from time to time I would look up, and the cloud movements continued through the whole show. It stands to reason that they charge so much.

Tuesday I was so insistent that I finally convinced Massa to take me to a revue, we ended up at the Maipo, they were doing *Good-by Obelisk*. I have the playbill here, with Pepe Arias, his wife Aída Olivier whom I didn't know because she doesn't act in the movies, she's a very good dancer, the tango singer Sofía Bozán who is marvelous, blond Alicia Barrié, and that pretty dark girl who's always playing the other woman, Victoria Cuenca. How strange it was to see them in person! But I was sorry I went, it was all dirty jokes and I didn't know where to hide first. To top it off they even got in jokes about newlyweds, boy was I in a sweat! Then Wednesday we saw at the National theater Muiño-Alippi's company in *Papa's Ranch*, very good, with a country banquet at the end, in the playbill it said eighty persons on stage, I think there were. Last night they raved so much to my husband about the Italian puppets that we went, but it was in a neighborhood theater, the Phoenix, in the Flores district, which is on the way to Vallejos. I won't tell you, Mabel, how sad it made me to think that in a few days we're going to take that road . . . to the end. How ungrateful you'll say, living your whole life in Vallejos and now you don't want to come back. But, Mabel, what did Vallejos give me? nothing but heartbreak. I kept the Italian puppets playbill for you, truly divine, I'll tell you all about it when I get back. And tonight if I tell you, you won't believe me, you know who's making a debut in the Smart theater in a play that's called *The Women?* None other than Mecha Ortiz. I immediately thought of you, since she's the only Argentine actress that you can stand. If we can get tickets we're going tonight without fail, here at the hotel they telephoned and they said they're not reserving them, but if I miss it I'll simply die. The doorman says that movie stars are going, that it's an important premiere.

Well, Mabel, if we could only go see it together, I only hope that you're well and that your papa doesn't let what's happening to him get him down too much, business is not everything, Massa says. He says that's why at night you've got to have a good time, and forget everything, of course if it was up to him he'd stay here and have dinner and then to sleep right after, but I'm starting to get the knack of taking advantage of nighttime to see all the things there are to see in this dream of a town. Tomorrow Massa wants to see Camila Quiroga in *With Broken Wings*, he goes for serious dramas in a big way. I don't as much, for that life is enough, right?

As you see I've kept my promise. See you soon.

Much love,
Nené

She looks at her wristwatch—her parents' gift on the day of her engagement—and verifies that it will be several hours before her husband returns. She's pleased to think of all that she'll be able to do, in total freedom, without anybody controlling her, in a city like Buenos Aires. She looks in the newspaper to find the address of the Smart theater. On the headlines of the first page she stops without meaning to: "ITALY AND GREAT BRITAIN STILL DISAGREE OVER WITHDRAWAL OF VOLUNTEERS FROM SPAIN—In London the withdrawal of ten thousand men ordered by Mussolini is considered insufficient. London (Reuters). Yesterday afternoon . . ." She thinks of the fact that her father will surely read that news, when the newspaper reaches Vallejos, the next day.

He is sick and reads all the news from Spain. The joy of knowing that she married well will possibly help him through his illness. Noises in the lock are heard, she's pleased to think that it might be the maid—such amiable company—to change the towels as she usually does at that hour. The maid is the only woman she can talk to in Buenos Aires, always surrounded by men. But instead she sees her husband come in, smiling and unknotting his tie. She looks at him and upon realizing that he is preparing to take a possible siesta, without wasting time she asks him for two aspirins to ease a bad headache. He removes his billfold from a pocket where it is his custom to keep a package of aspirins.

TENTH EPISODE

A woman's lips set the frozen north
aflame.

(tag line for *Northern Pursuit*,
starring Errol Flynn and Julie Bishop)

—Hello . . .

—It's Fanny!

—Hello? Who is this?

—It's me, Fanny! Is Mrs. Nené around?

—Yes, but who's this?

—It's me, Fanny! Big Fanny, is this Nené?

—Yes, it's me, how are you Fanny? It's late, ten thirty
already, you scared me.

—I've come to work in Buenos Aires, don't you remember me?

—How could I forget, is your baby with you?

—No, I left him with my aunt in Vallejos, she doesn't
work as a maid anymore, she takes in laundry like I did so
she's in her own house all day long, and she's keeping my
baby there with her.

—How many months old is your baby?

—Not even, it's only a week since I saw him last, but I
can't stand being away from the little fellow, Mrs. Nené.

—No, I asked you how many months old he is, if he's
a year old yet.

—Oh, yes, when his birthday comes around and I'm
still here I'm going to go see him. . . .

—You don't understand me, where are you calling from?

—The telephone in the bar on the corner, and they're all talking out loud.

—Cover one ear with your hand, that way you'll hear better, try it.

—All right, I'm doing just as you say, Mrs. Nené.

—Fanny, silly, don't call me missis.

—But you're married now.

—Tell me, how many months old is the baby?

—He's going on a year and three months.

—What's his name again?

—Panchito, do you think I was wrong to give him that name? You know why . . .

—What do I know, Fanny? . . . Did you ever see him again?

—He's building a house the same place he has his shack, he's building it all by himself, you know Nené that Pancho is a hard worker, he wants to first build his house before getting married or anything, he works like a horse, after finishing up his officer work he goes home to build the house.

—And when it's finished did he promise you anything?

—No, nothing, he doesn't want to talk to me anymore because he says I've been telling everybody that he's the little fellow's father. Because I had sworn not to say anything to anybody until he was sure of his job on the police force.

—And is it true you've been telling everybody?

—Not me or my aunt have said a thing. And aren't you expecting?

—There seems to be something . . . but tell me about Vallejos, did you see mama?

—Yes, Mrs. Nené, I saw her on the street, she was

with your papa, who still looks thin, why does he walk so slow like that?

—He's very sick, Fanny, it looks like he's going to leave us soon. He has cancer, poor papa. Was he very thin, Fanny?

—Yes, poor man, skin and bones.

—Where were they going, do you know?

—To the doctor, I think . . . and your mama gave me your telephone.

—Oh, it was her.

—And she asked me to see if you would answer her, Mrs. Nené, about sending the money or not. Your mama told me that you bought your living room set and that's why you don't want to send her the money.

—And have you seen Celina? who's she going with?

—I don't think she's going with anybody, they say she always goes out the door of her house at night, and someone always passes by and starts talking to her.

—But do they know anything for sure?

—They all say that Celina is easy, but nobody's knocked her up. When they knock her up people aren't going to say hello to her the same as they did with me.

—And have you seen Juan Carlos?

—Yes, he's always wandering around. He never does any work. And now they say he's going with the DiCarlo widow again. Didn't you know?

—Who told you?

—Well . . . everybody says so. Can't I come to your house to visit someday?

—Of course, Fanny, you must come visit sometime, but not without calling first.

—Okay, I'll call you, if you're not going to throw me out because of what happened to me.

—What are you saying?

—You know, that I didn't get married and I have a child already.

—Don't be silly, Fanny, it makes me angry when you say those things. Now when you come, I'll tell you a thing or two about that scoundrel.

—Which one? Juan Carlos or Doctor Nastini?

—No, the scoundrel who got you in trouble.

—You think he did it on purpose? Couldn't it be that he's afraid they'll throw him off the police force if he marries someone like me?

—I'll wise you up, Fanny. You call me next week and we'll talk. Call me up someday again, Fanny.

—Yes, missis, I'll call you.

—By, Fanny.

—Thank you, missis.

Nené sits still on the bed a moment waiting to hear her husband's footsteps behind the closed door. The silence is almost total, the trolley car on the street runs along its rails. She opens the door and calls to him. There is no answer. She goes to the kitchen and finds him reading the newspaper. She reproaches him for not having answered her. He in turn complains that she always bothers him when he's reading the newspaper.

*

—Hello . . .

—It's Fanny.

—Hi, what's new?

—Who's this, Nené?

—Yes, how are you doing? where are you calling from?

134

—From the same telephone in the bar, and your husband?

—Fine. The other day we talked about so many things and you didn't even tell me where you're working.

—In a factory, Nené. I don't like it, I want to go back to Vallejos.

—Where are you living?

—In a room, with my aunt's friend who brought me here. She's been working since last year in the soap factory. Couldn't I work for you instead?

—Here in my house you mean? No, when I have kids, then I'll need help, but not now. My husband doesn't even come home for lunch on workdays.

—Would you like me to visit you?

—Not today, Fanny, I have to go out. But someday I want you to come, so you'll see the house. A pity mama can't see the house, with the new dining and living room sets, few in Vallejos have a home like mine, mama wouldn't believe her eyes.

—My aunt's friend went somewhere today since it's Sunday with another old lady like her who doesn't like me, they invited me to come but the other one always laughs at my not knowing how to cross the street, for *that* I'd rather stay home alone.

—My husband went to the stadium to see the game, but later I'm going to see if he can take me somewhere, if not I'd tell you to come.

—And for a little while now? What time is he coming?

—No, Fanny, because if he sees you here later he's going to think that I already did something on Sunday and he won't want to go out.

—Where's he going to take you?

—To the movies or the theater, the main thing is that I

135

don't want to make dinner, I'm tired of cooking every night and hitting the sack right away.

—Where is your house? is it far from me? If you want to come here, mine is the room that has a big pot with a thorn bush in front, there are some big plants in the court-yard . . . and we can make maté. And I'll cut a branch off the thorn bush for you.

—No, Fanny, thanks but my husband doesn't want me to go out alone.

—And I'll tell you all about Miss Mabel . . .

—What did she do?

—Nothing much, just that before I left, her boyfriend came to visit, he came from Buenos Aires to see her. He's short, the same height as Miss Mabel, she has to wear low heels now.

—Are they engaged?

—No, if so she would have already been telling every-body, because after that trouble Mr. Saenz had they don't have much to brag about anymore. And do you want me to tell you something about Doctor Nastini?

—Fanny! I don't even remember that scoundrel.

—And your husband didn't say anything to you?

—About what?

—Oh . . . nothing.

—Tell me more about Mabel, what does her boyfriend do?

—When Miss Mabel was here in Buenos Aires the mis-sis told me that she had met a boy who was courting her but Miss Mabel didn't like him, he didn't have character, she said.

—Do you remember if the boy was a teacher?

—Yes, I think so since Mabel said he had a woman's job. . . . And as long as I could still nurse the baby I stayed in Vallejos, as much as my aunt told me to, I wouldn't come.

He will be warm enough now that winter's starting, won't he?

—Of course, why shouldn't he be? . . .

—Nené, I want so much to see Panchito. When did you last see him?

—When he was a month old.

—And you didn't come to the shack anymore, neither you nor Miss Mabel came anymore, I kept waiting for you and you never came back. And your husband, where's he going to take you?

—I don't know, Fanny. Besides I'm not even sure we're going out, you call me soon, Fanny, some other day, okay?

—And did you send your mama the money? Because I didn't say anything but your mama told me the whole thing.

—About what?

—That first you said you'd pay for your father's treatment in the sanatorium, and now they have to go to the town hospital.

—But mama told me they took just as good care of him in the hospital, and as much as I'd like to I can't because I got into the damn living room expenses. And just the same she moved him back to the sanatorium afterward, on her own sweet will, that you don't know. So let her take the money out of the bank, isn't that, by the way, what savings are for, for necessities?

—She told me that you were bad to your papa, and that she wasn't going to write you anymore. Did she write you?

—Of course she wrote me.

—And when am I going to see you?

—Call me soon. By, Fanny.

—By.

Despite her headache and increasingly bad mood she sets about making the bed, for the second time that day, like every Sunday. Her husband unmakes the bed after lunch, on Sundays and holidays, to lie down before going to the soccer game, a fact which provokes arguments not only related to the inconvenience of remaking the bed. Nené reflects and tries to resign herself, thinking that he only comes home for lunch on Sundays and holidays.

*

—Hello . . .

—It's Fanny! is that you?

—Yes, how are you? . . . Oh, Fanny, thank you so much for the present you brought, I was sorry not to be here that afternoon, I had just happened to go out, and I go out so little. But I had already told you to call me before coming.

—I wanted to give you a surprise. Did you like the branch?

—Yes, when I came in I saw it. Later the janitor's wife told me she had opened the door for you.

—She didn't want to open the door, she didn't want to at all, but I told her it was a delicate branch, and that if you don't plant it right it dries up. Do you like where I put it?

—Yes, it looks like it's doing well.

—I'm going back to Vallejos. I'm going tomorrow.

—Why? What happened? don't you go telling mama you saw my house!

—I got enough together now for the ticket and today was my last day of work in the factory.

—And what are you going to do there? take in wash again?

—No, Miss Mabel said to my aunt that if I wanted to come back she'd take me on again, since now that they can't have a cook and a maid, me and the mother are going to do everything. And they'll let me go see Panchito every afternoon.

—And didn't you get yourself any boyfriend here?

—No, I'm afraid to get mixed up with men I don't know.

—Are you going to tell mama you came to my house?

—If you don't want I won't tell her anything.

—What time does the train leave tomorrow? Because if you like I'll bring you some used clothes of mine.

—It leaves at ten in the morning. But better still if you have something new for Panchito. He needs it more than me.

—Well, I'm not going to have much time, but if I find something I'll buy it for him. But meanwhile I'll see you tomorrow without fail at the station. You go early, that way you'll get a good seat.

—Make sure you come, and if you have something old for me don't forget that either.

—Fanny, promise me that you won't tell Mabel either that you saw my house.

—I promise, and would you happen to have a shawl for Panchito for the cold?

—I'll see. By, Fanny, I have things to do.

—Okay, see you tomorrow.

—By, and get there early.

—By.

She again regrets having ordered a white telephone, always marked by fingerprints. Besides she needs a chair in that room so she won't have to sit on the bed each time she answers the phone. She decides to shine the ironwork on the bedroom set that very day. Going toward the kitchen she crosses a room intended to be the dining room where there's only a cardboard box containing a lamp with a white tulle shade. In the small foyer, intended to be the living room, there is also no furniture; she looks at the empty space wondering if she'll ever raise enough money to buy everything for cash, so that she can avoid the extra charges for interest in installment plans.

*

—While you're there, could you cut me some figs? *green velvety skin inside the pulp of sweet red grains, I burst them with my teeth*

—Hello, I didn't see you. *her foot, her painted toenails stick out of the sandal, skinny legs and a big rump*

—Hello.

—Forgive me for walking on this wall, but if we don't put up an antenna we won't hear the radio, and the prisoners are going to start complaining. *the prisoners never get to see a broad*

—And you too like to listen, don't deny it . . . *cheap half-breed bum, his neck and ears shine, he scrubs himself to pass for white*

—Why should I deny it? . . . Should I pick off the riper ones only, or the greenish ones too? *gabardine uniform and boots that shine*

—No, the ripe ones only, I'll come another day with a stick and knock down the ones that have turned purple. *I'll eat them all, one by one, and then I'll lie down in the garden, I don't care if crummy bugs in the grass bite me*

—Call me, I'll put the ladder on the other side and be on top of the wall in no time. *I'll climb up, jump down, touch her*

—And if you have something to do? or is listening to the radio all you do? *somebody knocked up a maid*

—It's no fault of mine . . . that there are no robberies. *a bullet, to blow my top off*

—Then I'm going to complain that someone's stealing my chickens. *long white feathers, black and yellow and brown curved feathers, the tail feathers shine, others fill a mattress, it's nice and soft, it sinks*

—They're not going to believe you.

—Why?

—Because you're right next door to the police station, that's one henhouse that couldn't be safer. *a white hen for the cock, there's no cocks in this yard, at night it's a fox that's going to get into the henhouse*

—A good thing, wouldn't you say? . . . A pity you can't put ants in prison, look how they're ruining my rose-bushes . . . *soft like velvet, fresh pink petals, they spread open, a man caresses the petals, smells their perfume, cuts the rose*

—What are you spraying them with?

—Poison for the ants. *little, black, bad ants, big dark bum, with bricklayer's arms, I wonder if he raped Fanny* Have you heard from Juan Carlos, you who were such a good friend of his?

—Yeah, he wrote me a letter . . . *Juan Carlos asks about a slut*

—But then again he never did take care of himself, and you were a good influence if I'm not mistaken . . . *which of the two is more of a man? which of the two has more brawn?*

—Juan Carlos was my best friend, and he'll always be the same for me. *the bricklayer has a brick house, and is his broad a schoolteacher?*

—Where is he? in that same plush sanatorium as be-

141

fore? *he would half close his light brown eyes when he'd kiss me*

—No, in a boardinghouse, I think, and he goes to the doctor on the side.

—That other sanatorium was very expensive.

—Yes, it seemed to be. . . . Shall I pull off these here?

—Those . . . yes, they're ripe enough now, have some yourself. *his big brown and yellow teeth*

—They're hard to skin. *I skin you, soft green skin, sweet red pulp*

—I'm afraid you might fall.

—I'm not going to fall, I'll throw them to you one by one, catch . . . here it goes . . . very good . . . did it burst? *the hens squawk, they cackle, flap their wings against the wire fence and bruise themselves, the foxes scram through any hole in the brick wall*

—Wait while I have a bite. . . . Tell me about the time you made friends with Juan Carlos. *a dark half-breed, he was white, his arms not so strong, his shoulders not so broad*

—One day when we were kids I challenged him to a fight. *where do she-foxes keep their lair? that you never can tell*

—And have you been with the police a long time?

—A year and a half since I came back from school in La Plata.

—And the girls must like your uniform, right? *Fanny's coming back from Buenos Aires, will the bum jump over the wall to rape her all over again?*

—No, that's a lot of bull. Who told you that? *the white girls yes, the housemaids are dark and hairy*

—I know that some girls have a weakness for uniforms. When I went to school in Buenos Aires my schoolmates were always falling in love with cadets. *a cadet, not any half-breed policeman*

—But you didn't? *you did, you did*

—*yes, I did.* No, I behaved, I was a good girl. And don't you go worrying about me because I have a fiancé, and for real. *a nice guy, a pygmy compared to some big husky bum*

—Who? the one who came from the capital this summer? *a runt I can land him on his ass with one blow*

—Who else do you think? . . .

—A kind of short guy . . . *she-fox, where do you keep your lair?*

—I'm the one who has to like him, not you.

—Want me to cut more figs?

—Okay, those higher up. *don't go yet* . . .

—*and the mother? where is she?* But I can't reach. I'd have to jump down to your courtyard and go up the tree, want me to?

—No, because if my mother sees you she's going to scold me, but if you like, some other time when you're at the police station and don't have anything to do, you can come down and climb up the tree, when my mother's around you'd better not. *mama never says anything, anything, anything, and Fanny's coming in a few days*

—But isn't your mama always there? *I'll catch the fox by her tail*

—Yes, mama's always here, she almost never goes out.

—Then . . . when can I come down? *at night, at night* . . .

—*at night, at night* . . . I don't know, mama's in all the time.

—Doesn't she take a siesta?

—No, she doesn't take a siesta.

—But at night she must sleep . . .*I don't make noise when I jump over the wall, the hens aren't going to wake up*

143

—Yes, but at night you can't see well enough to climb the tree. *a husky guy like him can climb a fig tree like nothing*

—I can see . . .

—But you can't see which fig is ripe, and which isn't. *come, come*

—Yes, because I touch them and the ripe ones are soft and let out a little drop of honey, and I'll eat them all up by myself if I come tonight. What time does your mama go to sleep? *I got her now and I won't let go*

—By twelve for sure she's asleep . . . *I wonder if he raped Fanny, is he as strong as that? Fanny comes and finds me with a dark half-breed bum*

—Then I'm coming tonight at that time. *the runt's fiancee*

—And is the antenna up? *I'm dying to kiss a real man, like your friend*

—There's time for that, first I'm going to eat a fig. *me walking down the street with the schoolteacher, for everybody to see*

ELEVENTH EPISODE

> The blind girl stared intently
> though still her eyes were blank
> as she listened to the clamor
> of the other girls at play . . .
>
> > (from Ramuncho's tango
> > "Little Blind Girl")

June 1939

White handkerchiefs, undershirts and underpants, white shirts on this side. This white shirt no, because it's silk, but all the others on this side, one scrub and into the tub, just one squirt of bleach. White sheets, I don't have any, the white petticoat, careful, it's silk: it'll fall to pieces if I put it in bleach. A light blue shirt, colored handkerchiefs, and checked napkins in this basin, and first all the undershirts and underpants because they're not colored, the white handkerchiefs and this brassiere, how am I going to get through the day without seeing my baby? but I know it's for his good, damn this water's colder than a witch's tit. One scrub in the wash tray, my aunt washes outside in the pump water at the shack and she dies it's so cold but here in Miss Mabel's laundry room I close the door and that keeps the wind out, if he's asleep when I come home tomorrow I'll wake up mama's Panchito! . . . Tomorrow afternoon I'll do the errands, and then the train all night long from Buenos Aires to Vallejos? how far Buenos Aires was from that little bugger of mine! tomorrow I'll do the errands and I'll walk the fifteen blocks, I'll give him the ball to play with and when I come back I'll wash the dinner dishes for the missis, the boss, and Miss Mabel: Panchito is just like his father, behind the brick wall Francisco Catalino Paez is in his uniform, what is he doing? he whips a prisoner and they all cringe with fear, until he finishes work, puts on his cape, and turning the corner a surprise awaits him. With this clothespin I hang one tip of the petticoat with the tip of the white silk shirt, another pin to the other tip of the shirt, and don't you touch the checked napkins, and tomorrow you'll all be dry, will it be cold on the street corner in my new dress? but the clothes hanging in the laundry room won't get black from dust. "What's your name?" they're going to ask Panchito. "My name is Francisco Ramírez, and I'm going to study to be a police officer," when his father's old his officer's job will go to his son for sure. But one day I'll be walking with Panchito on the street 'cause he already walks by himself, will he be bowlegged forever? I'll hold his hand, all these little buggers are bowlegged, but when they get bigger later on do their legs straighten up? I'll meet his father accidentally and if he's on the other side of the street I'll cross over and show him his son, of course Pancho's going to love him! he's the spitting image of him and then we get married any old day, no party, why spend money? so that Pancho will realize I'm back from Buenos Aires and in the morning after six o'clock Mass nobody's in church, and Pancho and me and the godmother and godfather will go in through the little back door, it's Mr. and Mrs. Saenz that I'll ask to be the godparents, since Mabel is at school in the morning, ". . . and the gaucho all in wonder, speaking softly to his saddle, said his gal would not come back . . ." it's a sad tango, because when his gal dies the gaucho is left alone with his horse and he feels so lonely ". . . surely God in His great wisdom took her with Him for all time . . ." and it doesn't say she left a child behind, if I die, Pancho would be left with Panchito, in whose shack? in his or my aunt's? we're alone in the room Pancho and me and with this pin I hang the blue shirt by a sleeve and the colored handkerchiefs are already hung so the only thing left is the white silk shirt so if I die he won't be so sad to be left with Panchito, at least I left him a healthy, handsome son ". . . then he went into the mud house, lit the candle in a daze, by the feet of Mary's statue, both with tears upon their face. Tell her please not to forget me, Virgin Mary full of grace, tell her only that my poor heart is but an empty place, surely God in His great wisdom took her with Him for all time . . ." and if I see him crying and praying for me, I'll forgive him everything! shouldn't I, blessed virgin? and when I get back from the street I'll take the clothes out of the bleach and one last rinse and it's all set: but if I die would he marry someone else? Well at least he'll have kept his promise and married me, and if I die it's no fault of his, it's God's will, how sad, the poor gaucho has nothing left but his horse, ". . . then he went into the mud house, lit the candle in a daze, by the feet of Mary's statue, both with tears upon their face . . ." and I'm really going to pray one day for Nené to be happy and have lots of children, she came to say good-by at the train and brought the material with her, lovely silk for summer, on the street corner in a square neck like Miss Mabel, will Panchito cry because I can't see him today? it's for your own good, mama's pet, look at mama in this mirror, do you like her in her new dress? ". . . I was happy in the sweatshop, felt no need to dance at all . . ." those girls in Buenos Aires make more money in the sweatshop but they'll get theirs just the same, let them laugh at me ". . . till the day a gallant wooer came to take me to the hall . . ." he must have been dark and handsome, when Pancho holds me so tight it's as if he'll never let me go . . . I wonder why her boyfriend left that girl in the sweatshop? this comb in my hair so the wind won't mess it up on the street corner, it's so cold I better wear my coat—right?—such an old coat ". . . my obsession, heartbreak tango, plunged my soul to deepest sin, as the music of that tango set my poor heart all a-spin . . ." a step, then a turn, he moves his leg forward and pushes mine, I'm not too good at dancing the tango, going backward all the time, he would go forward while my part was to go backward, his legs pushed my legs to go backward and when he'd stop for a second waiting to start up again in time with the music, it was real lucky he didn't let go of me because he'd suddenly stop dancing and I could have fallen on the floor, but he held me nice and tight, and the boyfriend left the girl in the sweatshop because she didn't have a new dress! ". . . oh such a lovely melody, it changed my destiny, my heart sang and bled that night . . . in the glow of candle-light . . ." her heart bled, she could have died and left her son an orphan, does she cry every night like me? but she doesn't die and leave her son, crying doesn't kill anybody ". . . with its music loudly drumming, and its fascinating thrill, I know my end is coming, yet it seems the world stands still . . ." they'll throw her out of the sweatshop and she'll have to go to work as a maid, ". . . I will always blame that tango, and the wooer with his wiles, once he'd made my heart break, all he told me was good-by . . ." the threadbare sleeves and the lapels, if I put on this coat he won't see that I'm wearing a new dress ". . . in the glow of candlelight my heart sang and bled that night . . ." she should get hers for being such a good-for-nothing! what do those girls in the sweatshops in Buenos Aires know about work, because they're in the big city they think they're better than maids, I'm never going to leave Miss Mabel's house! she lets me see my baby every afternoon and when I come back later today from the street the clothes in the pail are already whitened, will the coffee stains come out? and if they don't I'll scrub them again with soap, a good thing I remembered this shell comb, filthy nasty wind! and at seven Pancho will turn the corner as usual and he'll look happy to see me after such a long time, don't say I was naughty not to come wait for you before, it's just that I wanted to wear a new dress for you, I've been back from Buenos Aires for two weeks already! did someone tell you or didn't you know? Nené gave me the material, remember her? and Pancho asks me to take him to the baby and I tell him I can't because I haven't finished rinsing the whites but if he wants he can go now because my aunt's there with Panchito, is he going to like the name? he's very happy I gave the baby his name and God forbid I catch pneumonia, what if I had brought Panchito? I'd wrap him in the shawl that Nené Fernández gave me and he wouldn't have caught cold, that way his father could have seen him at last and we would go to church because I'm going to tell him the baby's not baptized yet, than Pancho will believe the lie and we'll go to church to baptize him, and there he finally decides and we get married once and for all. Uniform, boots, cap, but he's fat, the chief of police! is it seven o'clock already? is he coming to put me in prison because I had a child without being married? and the material was given to me, does he think I stole it? the chief of police is going into the coffee shop! and if he arrests me some day I'll tell him all the houses I worked in and let him speak to the missis and Miss Mabel, why is Pancho taking so long to come out? ". . . one cold morning I was strolling, saw the blind girl in the park, at her side was an old woman, as her comfort and her crutch . . ." is my slip hanging down? Miss Mabel didn't tell me that the dress was lopsided! ". . . the blind girl stared intently though still her eyes were blank as she listened to the clamor of the other girls at play . . ." Celina, Mabel, and Nené played, until sixth grade, they'd jump rope during recess ". . . then I heard her plaintive murmur as she asked her once again, why is it dear old woman, why is it I cannot play? . . ." my aunt has hair on her legs and a mustache too, if she shaved it would come out thicker each time, and dark hands, and green varicose veins, but the mayor's maid happens to be white, so what, Pancho too is dark, like everybody who lives in the shacks ". . . Lord! my child! you poor poor darling! Come with me was my reply, then I kissed her on the forehead and she had a playmate now . . ." and the blind girl's father? one day he walks by the square and shuns her, and the old woman doesn't have the strength because she's too old to stick a knife into that bad man, but don't worry the good woman came to help the old lady ". . . so it happened then that daily they would meet me in the park, and the blind girl's little fingers would reach out with love for me . . . she was innocently happy as she sat and played again, her caresses were a blessing on the three of us at play . . ." and as soon as we're married the baby plays in a nice white crib and the father comes home to bed completely tired, he did his officer work, and then he made a pit to start the wall for the bathroom of the little house, he washes in the cold water from the pump but soon he'll have the shower, and Pancho throws himself on the bed tired but clean, and Panchito in his crib stands up by himself and looks, holding on to the rail, what do I care if there's no kitchen in the shack! first let Pancho have the satisfaction of building the brick bathroom, when he can he'll make the kitchen but for the time being I'll wash the dishes and pots outside, I'll throw the leftovers if there are any to the chickens and when I go back into the room how tired I'll be, and the two of them will be playing, ". . . yet a day I well remember, the old woman came to tell me the blind girl was close to death . . . I went running to her doorway! Will you have someone to play with? as she died she asked this question, and Don't leave us I replied . . ." and that good woman who plays with the blind girl sees the father go by one day and asks him why doesn't he love his little blind girl, my it's hard to say, is he good or just plain bad? ". . . can I ever now forget you? my own child was just like you . . . young and innocent and blind, and she had no one to play with . . ." now, mama's pet, don't you get sick . . . eat all the food that your old auntie gives you, 'mmm good, that's it, my pet, eat it all up so you won't get sick in this cold . . . I'd rather be blind first, before my baby is, I'll go and throw undiluted bleach right in my eyes, I'll become blind and then Pancho feels sorry for me and marries me, my aunt takes care of the meals ". . . and my eyes were like two mirrors where all joy had found its place . . ." bleach burns when it gets into your eyes ". . . night grew cruel, they were blinded, crystal splinters in the dark . . ." will windows break into pieces? goose-flesh from coming out without a coat ". . . my eyes were veiled by fog, I was lost in search of you . . . and in my black and lonely dusk I can only weep for you . . ." do blind people cry? do tears come out of those people missing an eye? and how about the ones who have a glass eye? ". . . a hundred stars that throb and pulse, memories glisten in my heart . . ." I'm not going to leave you, Fanny, I promise I'll never leave you, I'm a bricklayer and I'm a good hardworking boy ". . . they give me hope, mirages of dawn . . ." I love you, Fanny, I love you forever ". . . in the sad night of blinded souls . . ." he takes advantage of my blindness and brings another whiter one home, the mayor's maid, and he tells me she's an old woman ". . . and my eyes were like two mirrors where all joy had found its place . . . night grew cruel, they were blinded, crystal splinters in the dark . . ." broken glass splatters, a pointy splinter, the girl in the sweatshop bleeds: a big piece of glass cut into her like a knife does meat, it passed through her ribs and split her heart in half! and with one chop I cut the wing off a plucked chicken, the head, the feet, I took his liver and his heart out, a chicken's heart is little, and I plucked a hen, I cut right into her and inside she was full of tiny eggs, boiled in oil and salt Miss Mabel's mother likes them, is a hen's heart bigger than a chicken's heart? and I don't mind if you don't apologize, I know that you can do better, find a girl who's not a maid, and what if when he comes by he doesn't look at me? and what if he gets angry and spits at me? the boots and the cap . . . here he comes! in his new cape! and my dress is all lopsided! Pancho, just look at the top of me, the square neck and the short sleeves, don't look at the lopsided fringe and my slip that's hanging down, why is he crossing the street? didn't he see me? yes, he saw me, Pancho! he went straight into the coffee shop! is he friends with the chief of police? our son is going to be blind! and I'll grab the bleach and throw it all over me and burn myself, because I was bad and didn't take care of my baby, blind and fatherless, one day he fell out of the crib and from not knowing how to stand on his two little bowlegs he split his forehead open; his little head split in two and he died on me, that's what the punishment is going to be! 'cause his father will repent when it's too late, he'll have to go back to the shack all by himself, where if there's a lighted candle he'll pray to the holy virgin, his wife died on him, and his son died on him too, will the clothes be whitened by now so's I can take them out of the pail? no, that'll take a little while longer, so should I go see the baby? and then come running back the fifteen blocks to take the clothes out of the bleach! and today my little bugger we're not going to have time to play because I'm behind, but tomorrow afternoon mama's going to bundle you up in the new shawl and take you right to the square, so you'll see the cars go by 'cause I know you like to look at them, and one day I'm going to take you to see the canaries in Mabel's cage, and another day, when I get paid, I'll buy you the little shoes, does the shoe store close at seven thirty? and your papa didn't say hello to me because he was in a hurry, was he going to the shoe store to give us a surprise? I'm afraid you're going to be bowlegged forever from walking without shoes, but all the little buggers like you are bowlegged, until they're two years old, Panchito, how many more blocks until I can give you a kiss? my poor little bugger, don't you have a father? I promise you that when I get paid I'm going to buy those shoes, and if your papa sees us and walks by sometime somewhere and in front of everybody he dares shun you . . . he better watch out! did he cross over to the coffee shop because he was afraid I'd go and stick a knife in him? . . . with the big kitchen knife I chopped the wing, neck, feet off a plucked chicken, I took his liver and his heart out, to fry them in the pan, every piece has to be thrown into the pan already cut, but not when you do roast chicken, then all I have to do is run after him in the henhouse, I grab him, stretch his neck, and with one blow I cut off his head, his wings keep flapping a while after his head is cut off, and his eye blinks, I pull off all his feathers and with all my strength I slice into him again to open his breast, I tear out all the garbage inside that you throw away, turn on the faucet and wash him under the jet of ice cold water . . .

June 1939

. . . the ripe fig, its green skin has no taste, inside the red pulp with its drops of honey, I ate all I wanted, down the hatch, the dolls on the shelf, natural hair and eyes that move, if I want I can twist their arms, legs, head, until they hurt because at night dolls can't scream, the three banners, the wooden cross, and the bronze Christ, the picture frame, the bureau, the wardrobe, the perfumed pillow case, my black head on the white pillow, the sheet is embroidered with fake flowers and a frilly fringe links them together from one tip of the bed to the other, the wool blanket cropped off some tame little sheep, she lets the billy goat come near her: the life-sized doll is all covered up, I wake her up when I want to, in the dark her black hair and mouth, the dolls sitting on the shelf, they don't move, I twist them around and turn their heads, their arms, legs, they can't scream because the father will come and see me: I twist one arm, I twist the other arm, they can't stand the pain any longer but if they shout they're discovered, the half-breed's dark skin smudged your embroidered sheets? he smudges your mouth and ears and your whole body from twelve at night till three, four in the morning, did he smudge your conscience? don't you have any regrets? these darn socks are sweaty, where's my undershirt? I dunk the rag in shoeblack and when it's daylight I smear it on my leather boots, I brush them with the shoe polish, dry already the shiniest boots in the world, I shine my belt too, she should shine it for me, lazy thing, the doll sleeps, the natural hair and the eyes that move, wake up, I'm going now, you have to close the window after I jump, it's cold out, the moon and the stars, the courtyard, my boots are going to shine, that little mouth of yours, it tastes like assorted candy, lemon, honey, eucalyptus, tomorrow you're going to give me more candy, tonight the toads are going to freeze in the ponds, and the water in the pipes too, they'll burst. The moon makes my boots shine! the toads, the pond, the grapevine, the maid is sleeping, the planters, the rosebushes, the ants, the dew, the frost, the fig tree, the ground, the grass, the brick wall, this moon makes my buckles shine, my metal buttons, a cat, I'm trembling, from the cold, there's a cat . . . nothing's there . . . who's stepping on dry leaves? . . . it's from the cold that I'm trembling, I'm not afraid of anybody . . . there's a cat around . . . don't you come near me! . . . I thought you were a cat, there's something shining in your hand, pointy cat claws? the kitchen knife . . .

Dearest:

You're going to think it's strange that I'm answering so soon. I got your letter today with the bad news and I couldn't beleive it, the poor guy. We were good freinds even though at one time he was just a half-breed bum. But you don't give me any details, please write and tell me how it all hapened as soon as you can. What a comotion there must be in town.

That's great about that guy wanting to buy the house, don't let him out of your sight, sell and come to me as soon as you can. I still haven't begun to ask the prices of real estate around here, I'm just a lazy bum and there's nothing to be done about it, but I'm sure you'll be able to get a good deel, and the important thing is we'll be together. I'm sick and tired of this shaby boardinghouse.

See what life is, that poor boy was briming with good health and now he's dead. I tell you I'm much better now, today I had about a four hour siesta and when I woke up the sheets were completly dry, instead of sleeping poorly and having bad dreams because of that news, because the more nervous I am the more I sweat, but not today. You see, I'm getting better.

A kiss and a hug for my pumpkin.

Juan Carlos

He puts down the pen, stands up, and opens the window to change the stuffy air in the room. He sees himself in the glass, smiling for no reason. He looks at his wristwatch, it's five o'clock and the sky is black, in the dark the mountains can't be seen. He thinks of the dead and of the possibility that they can observe what the living do. He thinks of his

155

dead friend who perhaps is looking at him from an unknown place. He thinks of the possibility that the dead friend realizes that instead of making him sad, the news of the murder has cheered him up.

TWELFTH EPISODE

> I wish I could say I was sorry.
>
> (tag line for *The Letter*,
> starring Bette Davis)

POLICE DEPARTMENT OF THE PROVINCE OF BUENOS AIRES

Station or Precinct: Vallejos.
Records Sent to: Lower Court of the Justice Department for the Province of Buenos Aires and local files.
Date: June 17, 1939.

PRELIMINARY RECORD (Extracts)

On the eighteenth day of the month of June of the year one thousand nine hundred and thirty-nine, the undersigned Police Captain Celedonio Gorostiaga, under the authority of Lieutenant Benito Jaime García who countersigns for all legal purposes, testifies that in this act the preliminary investigation corresponding to the bloody deed in which Police Officer Francisco Catalino Paez, ex-official of this police station, lost his life, is hereby established.

The deed was perpetrated on the morning of the seventeenth day of the present month of June, as attested by the sergeant on duty, Domingo Lonati, who heard screams while in the kitchen of the police station, located at the rear courtyard of the building. Said screams arose from a neighboring lot, but he could not determine precisely where at that moment, since the windows of the police station were closed owing to the low temperatures prevailing throughout the District of Vallejos in recent days, so when the sergeant went out into the courtyard, the screams had ceased and only a moan could be heard which also ceased. The sergeant climbed the brick wall taking advantage of a ladder he found placed against the wall, and looked toward the courtyard of the lot occupied by the living quarters of the resident neighbor Mr. Antonio Saenz. In said courtyard there is a large fig tree which hid the total view from him, but he thought he saw objects moving beside the door to the laundry room of said house. Sergeant Lonati thought it could be animals fighting such as cats and dogs and despite the low temperature he remained posted upon the wall as a lookout. A few minutes later he saw lights go on in the laundry room. He saw several persons moving and then the sergeant, shouting at the top of his lungs, offered his aid but nobody answered him because the door to the laundry room was already evidently closed. Sergeant Lonati thought it best to return to the guard duty office just in case the telephone rang and in fact before reaching the office the bell was already ringing. It was Mister Sáenz, summoning the aid of the police since Officer Páez lay on Mr. Saenz's property, now definitively lifeless, as the medical examiner later corroborated.

Immediately afterward the undersigned, Police Captain Celedonio Gorostiaga, residing on the top floor of the police station, was summoned by Sergeant Lonati and together they went over to Mr. Sáenz's household. The latter was waiting for them garbed in his night clothes and a bathrobe, the same as his wife, Mrs. Agustina Saenz, nee Barraza, and his daughter, Miss María Mabel Saenz. During their sleep they had been shaken by Officer Paez's screams, wounded in the garden by the household servant Antonia Josefa Ramírez, whom in the future we will refer to as "the accused."

[. . . testified that the body was already lifeless, and

pronounced him decedent for all legal purposes. The hospital attendant, with the help of the sergeant, transferred the stretcher contained in the ambulance to the above-named garden. Before removing the corpse, the undersigned had to impose his authority because the medical examiner insisted upon lifting the corpse without first allowing the undersigned to take the necessary measures, such as establishing in concise entries the position of the corpse in the precise place of its fall and also to take note of the state in which the surrounding plants were to be found, which in this case were rosebushes. The hospital attendant Launero, almost in contempt of the law, dropped the stretcher on the planter damaging the plants, but as the undersigned had already observed, the rosebushes which bordered the left-hand side of the path were intact, before the hospital attendant's intervention, while those on the right were damaged by the fall of the decedent. Therefore it can be deduced that there was no struggle to speak of, the officer was attacked from the front but without warning because otherwise it cannot be explained why he did not manage to take his revolver out of his holster, even though his right hand was grasping the handle of his revolver, which for fortuitous reasons he did not manage to unsheath.]

[. . . and here the lieutenant who countersigns the present preliminary investigation wishes to add that this proves that the first wound was in the abdomen, while that of the heart was administered when he was already on the ground . . .]

[. . . a stab from an eleven-inch-blade kitchen knife with a sharpened edge, which pierced him between the ribs straight to the heart, a blow which to tell the truth a woman could not have dealt the victim while in a vertical position, but could have in a horizontal position, which would permit the woman to thrust the knife down into an already by then defenseless body.]

[. . . and there she was lying unconscious on the bed. Keeping vigil, Miss Sáenz sat beside her. The accused was dressed only in a slip and underwear, the slip showed remains of bloodstains washed off with water but according to Miss Sáenz's explanation when they heard the screams they found the accused standing by herself beside the decedent, brandishing the weapon and stammering. Immediately thereafter she fainted and was led to her bed by Miss Saenz who was by then assisted by her parents. They placed the accused on the bed and washed her bloodstains with a sponge. As she was cold they covered her with her blankets and immediately proceeded to call the doctor and then the police, after which . . .]

[According to Miss Sáenz's statement, the accused had complained to her some days ago that the decedent (who had not spoken to her since he had learned of the pregnancy) had addressed her on the street ordering her to leave the door to the courtyard open so that he could enter at night to visit her, to which the accused reacted contemptuously since due to the lack of interest on the part of the decedent for his son she felt great resentment toward him. What happened that night on the other hand could not be explained in detail since the accused was found in the garden in a state of shock and had not explained anything.

Immediately thereafter, as his authority required, Dr. Malbrán examined the accused and found her without traces of sexual violence, but recommended not awakening her, so that she would come to naturally. It was then decided that Sergeant Lonati would remain in the room, while Miss Sáenz would also keep vigil over the accused, seated by the bed. It was immediately imperative to inspect the room arrangement, out of which it was concluded that there is access through only one door to the large courtyard, on either side of which door there are two windows: on the right the window of

Miss Sáenz's room and on the left the laundry room window, both windows sharing a garden view which ends at the wall bordering on the police station. According to Mr. Saenz said access to door was usually bolted shut but on more than one occasion it was left open, especially since the construction of the new police station, which afforded the occupants of the household a sense of security.]

[It was not until eight thirty of yesterday morning, that is the sixteenth day, that the accused woke up and was tended by Miss Sáenz. At nine forty-five Dr. Malbrán considered that the accused was able to respond to police questioning. The latter resulted in the following statements.

Antonia Josefa Ramírez, twenty-four years of age, confessed to having slain Police Officer Francisco Catalino Paez with a kitchen knife. The confession was interrupted several times by crises of tears and from time to time Miss Sáenz had to hold the accused down in her repeated attempts to knock her head against the wall. Miss Saenz, to whom the accused had already related the events as soon as she woke up, helped her to fill in the gaps constantly evinced by her memory. The deeds had been precipitated in the small hours of the sixteenth day when the accused saw the decedent enter her room, wearing his officer's uniform. The latter threatened her with his revolver and told her to yield to his wishes right there, despite the proximity of her employers. The accused, bearing much resentment for having been abandoned with an illegitimate son after having been seduced on the basis of empty promises, resisted and alleged to be afraid of waking up her employers, and as Miss Saenz opportunely vouched, it was Mrs. Saenz's custom to get up in the middle of the night with acid indigestion and go into the kitchen. Detail: said kitchen connects to the maid's room without a door, only a black cloth separates them, since said room was originally built as a pantry. With that argument the accused convinced the decedent to go out into the courtyard where she would do what he ordered. He didn't accept but the accused finally threatened to scream. Then the decedent, despite his drunkenness —this detail revealed in the autopsy—acceded and together they went out into the courtyard. But first they had to pass through the kitchen and it was there that the accused surreptitiously took the kitchen knife in passing and hid it. The decedent wanted to lead her to the back of the house, with the purpose of vexing her once again. When the accused, already in the courtyard, thought the opportune moment had arrived, she showed him the kitchen knife to frighten him away, but Páez, inebriated, didn't give the threat any importance, on the contrary . . .]

[. . . proceeded to investigate the birth certificate of the child Francisco Ramírez, born January 28, 1938, in the Regional Hospital of Vallejos, and upon it the father is noted down as unknown. Immediately thereafter, the accused's aunt, Miss Augusta Ramírez, forty-one years of age, profession laundress, was summoned. The latter under oath stated she had received money from Páez for the child's maintenance on more than one occasion, and added that on more than one occasion—that is every time she would see the decedent —she would bring the infant to him so that he could see him, under the condition, imposed by the decedent, that she would not tell the child's mother about him seeing him. According to the above-named laundress, he himself was very affectionate with his son because he looks a lot like him, and they would meet early in the morning in areas far from town, since the decedent was afraid of being seen with the child. Said decedent threatened not to give the laundress more money if she told the accused that he was seeing the child. On one occasion the decedent showed up with a rubber ball as a gift for the child, with the condition that the laundress would say that she had bought it with the money given by him, but the laundress preferred to tell the accused that she had found it on the street in a gutter since the accused would have considered that an excessive expense.]

[. . . in the laundress's neighbor's house, and was taken, along with the rubber ball, to the police station building to be observed by the officer who countersigns and by the undersigned. The resemblance to the decedent was pronounced as conclusive. As far as the ball is concerned, after urgent inquiry it was verified that it had been acquired in the Gaucho Inn General Store by the decedent at an undetermined date, between the past month of December and following January, perhaps for Christmas, as the owner of the store, Mr. Camilo Pons, stated under oath.

The investigation immediately proceeded to question certain neighbors for data concerning the accused's morals, and her former employers, the teacher Mrs. . . .]

[On the other hand a curious observation by Sergeant Lonati throws doubt on the unpremeditation of the bloody deed: he remembers having seen ex-officer Páez jump over the wall in the direction of Mr. Saenz's property another night, a few days ago, just as he remembers certain jests or jokes by the ex-officer about some presumed secret amusements on duty hours, jests which were never clarified and which nobody could elucidate. From this it can be deduced that the decedent might have already visited the accused other times, which would destroy the latter's alibi, although it can also be inferred that the decedent jumped over the wall but always found the access door closed, until, to his brutal punishment, he found it open yesterday morning.

Neither was it possible to find in the offices of the police station the receptacle of the alcoholic beverage imbibed by the decedent, which . . .]

With this data we consider the information gathered in reference to the case at hand complete. The accused is at present under medical supervision in cell no. 8 of this police station, incommunicado except for the medical examiner's necessary visits.

We attest to the present statement for all legal purposes.

CELEDONIO GOROSTIAGA
Police Captain

BENITO JAIME GARCÍA
Lieutenant

*

POLICE DEPARTMENT OF THE PROVINCE OF BUENOS AIRES

Police Station or Precinct: Vallejos.
Records Sent to: Local Files.
Date: June 19, 1939.

The minors under legal age, Celestino Páez, sixteen years old, and Romualdo Antonio Páez, fourteen, both brothers of the deceased ex-officer of this police station, Francisco Catalino Páez, were detained for throwing stones at Antonia Josefa Ramírez, arraigned for homicide, at the moment when the latter was boarding the train for the city of Mercedes, where a trial for homicide awaits her, accompanied by Patrolman Arsenio Linares. The defendant was hit by a stone and wounded at the base of her skull, though not seriously, but she was attended immediately by the first aid service provided by the same train, which left after a delay due to the above-named minors having hidden behind one of the coaches. As soon as they were apprehended the train left. Both minors remained at the disposition of the justice of peace for the District of Vallejos.

BENITO JAIME GARCÍA
Lieutenant in Charge

—May I? *she turns my stomach*
—Yes, please come in. I was waiting for you. *here's shorty all dressed up*

164

—You know how to keep plants, don't you? *but the house is nothing*

—It's the only thing I would regret leaving, if I leave Vallejos . . . *so stop staring at the broken floor tiles! dressed to kill, expensive wool coat, expensive felt hat*

—It's cold out, isn't it? *she doesn't even have heat, the poor slob*

—Yes, I'm sorry the house is so cold, come this way we'll go into the living room. *even if you wore white gloves you wouldn't find a speck of dirt here*

—Really, I don't mind going into the kitchen, if it's warmer . . . *no heater! double chin and bags under her eyes, she must be at least forty-five*

—Well, if you don't mind let's go, it's all clean, fortunately. *you thought you'd catch me with a dirty house, you midget! you're still a midget no matter how high a hat you wear to make yourself look taller*

—Does this stove use up much wood? *she must scrub it all day long, the ragpicker*

—Well, quite a bit, but since I'm here all day, it doesn't matter. *so I live simple, what business is it of yours?*

—Have you heard from your daughter? *that fatso*

—Yes, she's fine, thanks. *she caught herself a husband, not like you*

—Where is it she went to live, in Charlone? *stuck out in the sticks*

—Yes, the boy has a store in Charlone. It's so small, Charlone, isn't it? *but she's married, married, not a dried-up spinster like you know who*

—It's good that you're leaving Vallejos, what are you going to do here, alone? *and in the doghouse*

—Yes, my daughter's gone, what am I going to do here alone? *when you have a love, why waste time alone*

—How many years have you been a widow? *what*

could my brother have seen in her? she's common, dresses lousy

—It's been twelve years, already. The baby was eight years old when he died. I've suffered a lot in my life, Miss Celina. *and now it's my turn to have a good time*

—How old were you when your husband died? *confess*

—*what do I say?* The baby was eight . . . *no, no, no, no, I'm not going to give you that satisfaction*

—Now, as you may guess, I have something very important to talk to you about. *your short bob looks rotten and every ragpicker wears those hoop earrings*

—Yes, speak frankly. *God help me, this one's capable of anything*

—But first of all I want you to promise not to tell anybody. *miserable slob, you're going to have a tough time not blabbing the news to your neighbors*

—I swear to God. *will God punish me for swearing?*

—On whom? *if you swear on my brother I'll spit on you*

—*Juan Carlos I don't dare* On my daughter's happiness.

—Fine. Now, I got a letter from my brother telling me what you plan on doing.

—What does he tell you? *what's she getting at? is she going to threaten to tell my little girl?*

—What do you want me to repeat it for? *I fixed you*

—Well if he tells you something that doesn't happen to be true, I don't mean he's a liar, but just in case there's some misunderstanding. *just in case*

—He said that you heard that we, mama and I, *not you, you tramp* can't go on sending so much money to Córdoba for the new treatment, and that the boardinghouse he's at is not that good, and the best costs an arm and a leg, so you wrote him saying that you wanted to sell this house and move to Cosquín, to buy a little house there and take him on as a boarder. *how can my brother stand you, you old bag, in high heels and ankle socks all the time*

—Yes, that's all true, and if I can I'm going to take on real boarders to help with the expenses.

—Mama is very annoyed about all this. *about having to deal with ragpickers*

—Why? isn't it for her son's good? *all these prigs have hearts of stone*

—Yes, but she suffers because she can't help him the way she'd like to.

—*you'd do better to send him some pesos, instead of buying that felt hat of yours* Well, one shouldn't be so proud either, that's not good.

—Mama isn't proud, it is not right for you to say that. It just happens that my mamma was brought up to have all the comforts, and now it hurts, that's only natural, isn't it? *take that!*

—*you have some nerve to insult me, you bitch* Yes, mothers are like that.

—So therefore, mama, and I too, want to ask something of you.

—Tell me. *will she ruin everything? will I lose the one I love?*

—Are you going to sell your furniture, auction it?

—*am I saved?* No, because they won't give me anything for it, and later if I have to buy new furniture in Cosquín it's going to be very expensive. To top it off I don't even know if there'll be a furniture store there, and imagine what I'd have to pay if I went to the city of Córdoba?

—Mama and I figured that you were going to send the furniture from here.

—Yes, I'm sending it from here. And I got an offer for

the house already, did you know? *nothing, nothing is going to stop me*

—Well, mama, and I too, are asking you for one thing: You won't have any opposition from us, but we ask you not to tell anybody that you're going to Cosquín. *nervy old bag, going with a younger man*

—Don't worry, I wasn't thinking of telling anybody, and I'm not telling my daughter everything either. You know the big mouths they have around here. Just look what they say about Mabel . . . *there, take that, she's a friend of yours*

—*what are you trying to insinuate with that double chin of yours?* I don't believe it. A girl from a good family like Mabel wasn't going to get involved with that bum.

—*they're all tramps and you're the worst of all* It may just be stories. But it seems that in her testimony she contradicted herself.

—She was probably nervous . . . anyway, getting back to us, even if you don't talk about Cosquín, people are going to realize if you're not more careful. For example the furniture, don't send it from here.

—And how am I going to do it?

—If you send it by the moving van here, everybody will know right away. Send the furniture to your daughter's in Charlone, and from there to Cosquín. And take the same precautions for everything.

—*you won't take Juan Carlos away from me* What other precautions?

—Everything. So that nobody finds out you're there with my brother. You have to understand that it's a disgrace to our family. *I said it*

—*no, stealing is a disgrace* If God sent your brother that illness it was God's will, you don't gain anything by feeling disgraced.

—But do you promise to do that with the furniture

and the deed to the house? You have to give your daughter's address in Charlone for all transactions. Do you promise?

—I promise. *and you climbing into cars with traveling salesmen all the time, midget, what right have you to talk to me in that tone?*

THIRTEENTH EPISODE

> Her eyes of blue did open wide,
> my timeless grief she understood,
> and with a snarl of woman scorned
> said life plays tricks and left for good.
>
> (from LePera's tango "She Returned One Night")

It happened on an autumn afternoon. The trees that grew along that street in Buenos Aires bowed low. Why? Tall apartment houses on either side of the street blocked off the sun's rays, and the branches spread obliquely, as if pleading, toward the middle of the road . . . seeking light. Mabel was on her way to a friend's house for tea, she raised her eyes to the aged treetops, she noticed that the strong trunks bowed, humbly.

Perhaps a vague omen seized her throat with a silk glove, Mabel held a bouquet of roses in her arms and inhaled the sweet perfume, why did she suddenly think that autumn had come to the city never to leave it again? The front of the apartment building seemed luxurious, but the absence of a rug in the entrance reassured her: the building where she was very soon to live counted on just that decisive element to define its rank. Then again the elevator had a mirror, and she checked her makeup through the fine veil of her black felt headpiece, adorned with bunches of cherries, made from cellophane. Lastly she adjusted the fox tails wrapped around her neck.

Third floor, apartment B, in an upswept hairdo and

with so much shadow around her eyes that her friend Nene seemed somewhat aged when she opened the door.

—Mabel, how good to see you! —and they kissed each other on either cheek.

—Nené! What an angel, why the little darling is already walking! —she kissed the child and caught sight of her friend's younger son in a playpen—And the baby, what a cute face!

—No . . . Mabel . . . they're not cute at all, don't you think they're a bit homely? —the mother spoke sincerely.

—No, they're adorable, so chubby, with their little turned-up noses, how old is the youngest?

—The baby is eight months old, and the big one over a year and a half . . . but fortunately they're boys, right? it doesn't matter much that they're not cute . . . —Nené felt poor, she had nothing to show but two ungraceful children.

—But one after the other . . . you didn't lose any time, did you?

—You know, I was afraid you wouldn't have a chance to see me, how are the preparations going?

—Well, it's a madhouse, and I'm not even getting married in a long gown or having a party! . . . Your apartment looks so nice. —Mabel's voice crackled with hypocrisy.

—You think so?

—Of course I do! as soon as I come back from the honeymoon you'll have to come see my little nest, and for sure, my apartment is little.

—I'm sure it's a dollhouse. —Nené answered while placing the fragrant roses in a flower vase and admiring them— I'll bet you forgot to bring me a picture of your fiance.

Both thought of Juan Carlos's perfect face and for a few seconds avoided looking each other in the eyes.

—No, what for, he's just a runt . . .

—I'm dying to meet him, you're not marrying him for nothing, smarty. He must be a very interesting man. Show me the picture of the runt . . . —before finishing the last sentence Nené already regretted having said it.

—Such comfortable chairs. No! no, dear, don't touch my stockings!

—Luisito! You're going to get it if you don't stop . . . here, I'll get you a cupcake. —and Nene went into the kitchen to heat the water for tea.

—So you're Luisito, and what's your little brother's name? —Mabel smiled to the child searching his features for some decisive similarity to Nené's husband.

—Mabel, come, I'll show you the house.

Meeting in the kitchen the two couldn't escape the incursion of memories. All those afternoons spent in that other kitchen of Nene's, while outside the dusty wind of the pampas blew.

—You know something, Nene? I'd like a maté, like in the old days . . . how long has it been since we've had mate together?

—Ages, Mabel. Not since the time I was Miss Spring more or less . . . and here it is April of '41 . . .

Both were silent.

—Nené, one always thinks the past was better. And wasn't it?

They were silent again. Both found an answer for that question. The same answer: yes, the past was better because then they both believed in love. Silence followed silence. The dying light of dusk entered the window and tinted the walls violet. Mabel wasn't the hostess, but she couldn't stand the melancholy any longer, and without asking permission she turned on the light that hung from the ceiling. And asked:

—Are you happy?

Nené felt that a shrewder opponent had attacked her by surprise. She didn't know what to answer, she was going to say "I can't complain," or "There's always a but," or "Yes, I have my two sons," but she preferred to shrug her shoulders and smile enigmatically.

—It's easy to see you're happy, you have a family that not everyone . . .

—Oh, yes, I can't complain. What I'd like is a bigger apartment with a full-time maid, but to have one sleeping in the living room is more trouble than it's worth. You should see the work these kids make me. And now that winter's coming and they start with the colds . . . —Nené preferred not to mention her other complaints: that she had never set foot in a night club, that she had never traveled in an airplane, that her husband's caresses were not for her . . . caresses.

—Why they're healthy little things. . . . Do you go out a lot?

—No, where am I to go with these two always crying or going weewee or doing duty? Have kids, you'll see what it's like.

—If you didn't have them you would want them, so don't complain. —Mable, two-faced, figured that the routine life of mother and wife wasn't what she wanted either, but was it by any chance better to remain single in a small town and continue being the target of slander?

—And you, tell me about yourself . . . do you want a lot of kids?

—Gustavo and I have agreed not to have children until he graduates. He has a few more courses to go but he never takes them. I'll have to see to that. . . .

—What was it he's studying for?

—A Ph.D. in economics.

Nené thought how much more important a doctor in economics could be than a public auctioneer.

—Tell me about Vallejos, Mabel.

—Well, I don't have any fresh news, I've been in Buenos Aires more than a month, getting ready.

—Is Juan Carlos still in Cordoba? —Nené felt her cheeks blushing.

—Yes, it seems he's better. —Mabel looked at the blue flame in the gas stove.

—And Celina?

—Fair to middling. What's there to talk about, she went the wrong way, that's all. You know fooling around with traveling salesmen is fatal. Don't you listen to any serials in the afternoon?

—No, is there anything good on?

—Yes, a marvelous drama! at five, don't you listen to it?

—No, never. —Nené remembered that her friend had always been the first to discover the best movie, the best actress, the best leading man, the best radio serial, why did she always let her get one step ahead?

—I miss a lot of episodes but when I can I put it on.

—What a pity, today you'll miss it too. —Nene wanted to talk at length with Mabel, bring back old memories, would she dare to bring up the subject of Juan Carlos again?

—Don't you have a radio?

—Yes, but it's after five already.

—No, it's only ten to five.

—Then we can listen if you want. —Nene remembered that as hostess she must entertain her guest.

—Yes, marvelous! You don't mind? We can talk just the same.

—Sure, it's fine, what's the play called?

—*The Wounded Captain*, it has four days to go and next month they're going to do *The Forgotten Promise*. Want me to tell you about it from the beginning?

—Yes, but afterward don't forget to tell me about Fanny. How's she doing?

—Just fine. Well, I'll tell you the beginning because it's almost five and otherwise you won't understand a thing, and I'm sure you'll keep listening to it from now on.

—But hurry then.

—Well, it's during World War I, a captain in the French army, a young man, from a very aristocratic family, falls wounded somewhere on the German border, and when he comes to in the trenches he finds himself next to a dead German soldier, and hears that the place has fallen to the Germans, so he takes the uniform off the dead man so that he can pass for a German. And what's happened is that this whole region has fallen to the Germans and they march toward one of the villages around there, and pass a farm, and go in and ask for food. The farmer is a thickheaded, brutish peasant, but his wife is a very beautiful woman, and gives the Germans everything just as long as they keep moving on, but then she sees him and recognizes him. It so happens that she had been a girl from a village near the castle where the boy lived, and when he was just beginning his military career and would come home to the castle for holidays he would always meet her in the forests, she was his first love.

—But what kind of girl was she? Was she a good girl or the kind that sleeps around?

—Well, she had been in love with him since she was little, when he'd escape from the castle to go swimming in the brook and they'd gather flowers, and when she grew up she probably gave in to him.

—Then tough luck. If she gave in.

—No, in his heart he really loved her, but since she was a peasant girl, he had to give in to his family who wanted an arranged marriage with a girl of noble birth like him. But Nene, weren't we going to have maté?

—Oh, with the talk I forgot, the tea's already made, but you want maté, don't you? and does he love the aristocratic girl or not?

—Well . . . she's a young girl who is also very in love with him, and she's very refined, he must like her. Let's have the tea, forget about it. . . .

—But he can only truly love one.

Mabel preferred not to answer. Nené put on the radio, Mabel observed her and it was no longer through the veil of her hat but through the veil of appearances that she was able to see Nene's heart. There was no doubt about it: if the latter believed it impossible to love more than one man it was because she hadn't succeeded in loving her husband, since she had certainly loved Juan Carlos.

—And he goes back to her for convenience sake.

—No, he loves her in his own way, but really, Nené.

—What do you mean in his own way?

—Well, for him his country comes first, he's received many medals. And then came a part when her brother-in-law, a traitor, you get me? her brutish husband's brother, who's a spy for the Germans, comes to the farm and finds the boy hidden in the barn and the boy is forced to kill the spy and buries him at night in the orchard, and the dog doesn't bark because the girl has taught him to love the wounded guy.

"—LR7 Buenos Aires, your friendly station . . . presents . . . the 'Afternoon Radio Play' . . ."

—Meanwhile I'll serve the tea . . . the kids are hungry.

—Yes, but you have to listen, let me make it louder.

A melody on violin shed its first few notes. Then immediately the music's volume decreased and made way for the finely modulated voice of a narrator: "That cold winter morning, from his hiding place in the loft, Pierre could see the crossfire of the first shots. Both armies were confronting each other just a few miles from the farm. If he could only rush to the aid of his comrades, he thought. Suddenly there were noises in the barn, Pierre sat motionless in the hay loft."

"—Pierre, it's me, do not fear . . ."

"—Marie . . . so early."

"—Pierre, do not fear . . ."

"—My only fear is that this is all a dream, that I'll wake up and not see you anymore . . . there . . . against the light in the doorway, behind you dawn's rosy air . . ."

—Mabel, don't tell me there's anything more beautiful than being in love.

—Shsh!

"—Pierre . . . are you cold? The fields are covered with an icy dew, but we can talk freely, he has gone to town."

"—Why so early? doesn't he always go at noon?"

"—It's that he's afraid of not being able to go later on, if the battle spreads. That's why I've come to change your bandage now."

"—Marie, let me look at you. . . . Your eyes are strange, have you by chance been crying?"

"—What things you say, Pierre. I don't have time to cry."

"—And if you did?"

"—If I did . . . I would cry in silence."

"—As you've just done today."

"—Pierre, let me change your dressing, there, that's it, so I can remove the herb-soaked linen, we shall see if this coarse country medicine has done you any good."

"Marie proceeded to remove the bandages that covered her beloved's chest. Just as a battle broke out on the fields of France, so did two opposing forces strive in Marie's heart: more than anything she wanted to find the wound healed, as the joyful conclusion of her cares, though she had no faith in the healing power of those paltry rustic herbs; but if the wound was healed . . . Pierre would leave the place, he would go away, and perhaps forever."

"—This bandage has gone around your heart so many times, does it not hurt when I take it off?"

"—No, Marie, you can never hurt me, you are too gentle for that."

"—What nonsense you're saying! I still remember your screams the day I washed your wound."

"—But from your lips, Marie . . . I have never heard complaints. Tell me, how would you feel if I died in battle?"

"—Pierre, don't talk that way, my hands tremble and I might hurt you . . . I just have to remove the herb-soaked linen and that's it. Don't move."

"And, unbandaged, the decision of Destiny lay before Marie's eyes."

A lively and modern musical theme came on the air, followed by a commercial announcement describing a dentifrice of lasting and hygienic action.

—How do you like it, Nené?

—I do, the story is lovely, but she's not too good. —Nené was afraid to praise the actress's work, she remembered that Mabel didn't like Argentine actresses.

—Why no, she's very good, I like her. —Mabel replied, remembering that Nené never did know how to judge movies, theater, and radio.

178

—Did she give in to him for the first time in the barn or before when she was still single?

—Nené, before! can't you see that it's a love of many years?

—Of course, she can't have any illusions about him because she already gave in, because I thought that if she hadn't given in before when they were very young, and in the barn he was wounded and nothing could happen, then he would come back to her more eagerly.

—That has nothing to do with it, if he loves her he loves her. . . .

—Are you sure? What can she do to get him to come back to her after the war?

—That depends on the man, if he's a man of honor or not. . . . Quiet, it's beginning.

"Unbandaged, her destiny was written before her eyes. Marie saw with joy, with amazement, with sorrow . . . that the wound had healed. The ointment had produced the desired effect, and Pierre's robust nature had done the rest. But if Marie decided . . . that scar could open again, she had only to gently stick her nails into the new and tender, still transparent, skin which joined both edges of the deep wound."

"—Marie, tell me, am I healed? . . . why don't you answer?"

"—Pierre . . ."

"—Yes, tell me quickly, can I rejoin my troops?"

"—Pierre . . . you can leave, the wound has closed."

"—I'm on my way! I shall join my men, and then I shall return and if it is necessary fight him hand to hand . . . to free you."

"—No, never, he's a brute, a vile beast, capable of attacking from behind."

—Mabel, why did she marry such a terrible husband?

—I don't know, I missed a lot of episodes, it must be because she didn't want to stay single and alone.

—Was she an orphan?

—Even if she had parents, she'd want to make her own home, no? now let me listen.

"—How can you be so sure you are going to return?"

A lively and modern melodious theme came on the air, followed by a commercial for a toilet soap made by the same company advertising the already praised dentifrice.

—I'll kill you, Nene, you didn't let me listen, no . . . I'm only kidding. Look at me eat this cream puff! boy, I'm going to get fat!

—And Fanny? how's she doing?

—Fine, she didn't want to come back to work at our house anymore, she doesn't even look at me now, after all I did for her . . .

—And what does she live on?

—She takes in wash, at her shack, with her aunt. And the neighbor's wife died, he's a farmer with his own land, and the two women cook and take care of his kids, they get by. But she's ungrateful, Fanny is, those people, the more you do for them the worse they are. . . .

The narrator next described the state of the French troops. They were surrounded, they would gradually weaken. If Pierre joined them he would only increase the number of dead. But the astute captain thought up an extremely daring scheme: he would wear the enemy's uniform and sow confusion among the German lines. Meanwhile Marie confronted her husband.

—Would you be capable of such a sacrifice, Mabel?

—I don't know, I think I would have opened his wound, so he wouldn't go back to fight.

—Of course if he realized he'd soon hate her forever. There are times when you're up against the wall, right?

—Look, Nene, I think everything is written, I'm a fatalist, you can break your head thinking and planning and afterward everything comes out the opposite.

—You think so? I think that you have to play it to the hilt, even though it's once in your life. I'll always regret not having known how to play it to the hilt.

—How, Nene? by marrying a sick man?

—Why do you say that? why do you bring that up when I was talking about something else?

—Don't get angry, Nene, but who would have thought that Juan Carlos would end up like that?

—Does he take better care of himself now?

—Are you out of your mind? He spends his life chasing women. What I can't figure out is how come they're not afraid of catching it.

—Well . . . maybe some of them don't know. And since Juan Carlos is so handsome . . .

—It's because they're all dying for it.

—What do you mean?

—You should know.

—What? —Nene had the feeling that an abyss was about to yawn open, she reeled with vertigo.

—Nothing, I guess then you . . .

—Mabel, what are you talking about?

—I guess then you didn't have with Juan Carlos . . . well, you know what.

—You're terrible, Mabel, you're going to make me blush, of course there was nothing. But I don't deny that I loved him, as a boyfriend I mean.

—Come now, don't get like that, how edgy you are.

—But you were trying to tell me something. — Vertigo had taken over, she wanted to know what there was at the bottom of those abysmal depths.

—Well, it seems that when women have something going with Juan Carlos they never want to give it up.

—That's because he's so good-looking, Mabel. And so endearing.

—Oh, you don't want to understand.

"—If the French troops advance, we'd better leave here, woman. And faster with those bundles of hay and those molds of cheese. Each day you're clumsier, and now you even tremble with fear, blockhead!"

"—Where will we go?"

"—To my brother's house, I don't understand why he hasn't been back here."

"—No, not to his house."

"—Don't argue with me, or I will fetch you a blow upon your face, and you already know what a heavy hand I have."

—She lets him beat her! What a jerk!

—But Mabel . . . she must do it for her children, doesn't she have children?

—I think so. I'd kill anyone who dared hit me.

—How disgusting men are, Mabel . . .

—Not all of them, dear.

—Men who beat women, I mean.

The narrator took leave of the listeners until the next day, after interrupting the scene full of violent threats between Marie and her husband. The musical background followed and lastly another word of praise for the above-mentioned toothpaste and soap.

—But Mabel, what is it you're saying about Juan Carlos that I don't want to understand? —Nené continued playing with her own destruction.

—It's that women don't want to let go of him . . . because of things that happen in bed.

—But, Mabel, I don't agree. Women fall in love with him because he's good-looking. All that about bed, what you're saying, no. Because to tell the truth, once the light goes out you can't see if your husband is handsome or not, they're all alike.

—All alike? Then Nené, you don't know that there are never two alike. —Nené thought of Doctor Nastini and her husband, she was unable to establish comparisons, the moments of lust spent with the detested doctor had been fleeting and undermined by inconveniences.

—Mabel, what do you know, a single girl . . .

—Why, Nené, all my friends from school are married now, and we confide in each other completely, my dear, and they tell me everything.

—But what do you know about Juan Carlos, you don't know anything.

—Nené, you don't know the reputation Juan Carlos had?

—What reputation?

Mabel made a crude movement with her hands indicating a horizontal distance of approximately fifteen inches.

—Mabel! now you're really making me blush. —and Nené felt all her fears violently confirmed. Fears that she had harbored since her wedding night. What she would have paid to forget that vile gesture she just saw!

—And it seems that has a lot of importance, Nené, for a woman to be happy.

—My husband told me it didn't.

—Maybe he took you for a ride. . . . Silly, I'm pulling your leg, that's not what they told me about Juan Carlos, I only told you that to pull your leg. What they told me was something else.

183

—What?

—I'm sorry, but when they told me I swore I'd never, never tell anybody, I'm sorry.

—Mabel, that's not nice. Now that you began, finish it.

Mabel was looking in the other direction.

—I'm sorry, but when I make a promise I keep it.

Mabel cut a pastry in two with a fork, Nené saw that the fork was a trident, two devil's horns grew out from Mabel's forehead and under the table her winding tail curled around the leg of the chair. Nené made an effort and sipped some tea: the literally diabolic vision vanished and the hostess suddenly thought of a way of partially returning the blows dealt during the reunion and, looking her straight in the eyes, she asked abruptly:

—Mabel, are you really in love with your fiancé?

Mabel hesitated, the brief seconds she took to answer betrayed her game, the comedy of happiness was over. With profound satisfaction Nené confirmed that they were talking from one humbug to another.

—Nené . . . what a question . . .

—I know you love him, but sometimes one asks silly questions.

—Of course I love him. —But it wasn't true, Mabel thought that with time she would learn to love him, but what if her fiancé's caresses didn't make her forget the caresses of other men? what would her fiancé's caresses be like? for that she had to wait until their wedding night, because finding out before implied too many risks. Men . . .

—And you, Nené, do you love your husband more now than when you were engaged?

Tea, without sugar. Pastries, with cream. Nené said that she liked boleros and the Caribbean singers who had introduced them. Mabel voiced her approval. Nené added that they really got to her, the words seemed written for all women and at the same time for each in particular. Mabel affirmed that this happened because the boleros said many truths.

At seven Mabel had to leave. She regretted having to go without seeing her friend's husband—kept at the office for business matters—and therefore without appraising how much he had been disfigured by the many pounds acquired. Nené inspected the tablecloth, so difficult to wash and to iron, and found it clean, without a stain. Then she examined the satin chairs, they didn't have stains either, and she immediately proceeded to place their respective covers on them.

Mabel went out on the street, night had already fallen. As she had planned, she would take advantage of the free time before dinner to see the show windows of an important department store located in Nené's neighborhood, and compare prices. Mabel reflected, she had always been so organized, she had never wasted time, and what had she really achieved with all that calculation and precision? Perhaps she would have done better to let herself get carried away by an impulse, perhaps any man who passed her on that street could give her more happiness than her dubious fiancé. And what if she took a train to Córdoba? in the mountains there was the man who once had loved her, who had thrilled her as no one had. On that street in Buenos Aires the trees bowed low, both day and night. What useless humility, it was night, there was no sun, why bow? had those trees forgotten all dignity and pride?

As for Nené, she finished placing the covers on the chairs and cleared the table. Folding the tablecloth she discovered that a cigarette spark—Mabel being the only smoker—had made a hole in the cloth.

How careless, how selfish!—Nené mumbled to herself, and she would have liked to thrash on the floor, to utter a heartrending cry, but in front of her two children she could only raise her hands to her ears to still the haunting voice of Mabel Sáenz: ". . . and it seems that has a lot of importance, Nené, you don't know the reputation Juan Carlos had? . . . silly, I'm pulling your leg. What they`told me was something else . . . but when they told me I swore . . . I swore . . . I'd never, never tell anybody. And I only told you that other thing to pull your leg, Nené. WHAT THEY TOLD ME WAS SOMETHING ELSE."

Trees that bow day and night, lovely embroidered linens that a tiny cigarette spark can destroy, peasant girls who fall in love one day in the forests of France and who fall in love with someone whom they shouldn't. Destinies . . .

FOURTEENTH EPISODE

> It was the look in her eyes that made
> him think of murder.
>
> (tag line for *Woman in the Window*,
> starring Edward G. Robinson and Joan Bennett)

Father, I have many sins to confess   Yes, over two
years, I couldn't get up the courage to come   Because
I'm going to receive the sacrament of marriage, that was
what helped me to come   Yes, help me, Father, because I don't get anything out of feeling ashamed, help me
confess all I've done   I've lied, I've lied to my future
husband   That I had relations with only one man,
with a boy who was going to marry me and then got sick,
and it's not true, I'm deceiving him, what should I do,
Father?   But if I tell him I'm going to make him
suffer, it won't do anybody any good   But when
the truth only causes suffering, you still have to tell
it?   I'll do it, Father, but I have another big lie to
confess, it's such a big lie . . .   No, Father, the sin of
lust I already confessed, I'm cleansed of that sin already, another Father Confessor absolved me   I've lied before
Justice   Before the Lower Court of the Province of
Buenos Aires   No! I can't do that, Father
No, the truth would only make me and every-
one suffer more   Father, I'll tell you everything,
yes, you I can tell everything   Yes, Father
Why, Father?   I was living with my family in a town

in the province, and at night a man who worked in the police station would come into my room   No, Father, I wasn't in love with him   Help me, Father, I don't know why I did it   Yes, Father, it was to forget another man   Yes, Father, I loved the other one but he was sick and I left him, because I was afraid to catch it   He was trying to hide that he was spitting blood   I did him a good turn, Father, don't you think so?   At his side?   I don't know, Father. I did love him but when I saw that he was sick I didn't love him anymore. Father, I have to be frank, if not what am I here for? don't you agree?   Well, I wanted to have a house and a family and to be happy, Father, it's not my fault if I stopped loving him!   Yes, Father, I'm weak, and I ask forgiveness   That man I told you about would come to my room   No, not the sick one, the other guy, the policeman   No, the sick one wasn't a policeman. And one hot night when I left the window open I saw him looking at me from the garden: he had gotten into my house   No, I didn't have the strength to send him away, and he began to come when he felt like it, what should I do to be forgiven, Father?   No, I lied to Justice for another reason. It happens that this boy was the father of my maid's illegitimate son, and she came back from Buenos Aires when I had already fallen into temptation with him
No, she came back because I asked her to, or rather my mother did   No, she had worked for us before, when she got pregnant   No, I couldn't say anything to him because at that time I still didn't know him, I met him afterward, when he began to work for the police   No, not during the trial, I met him before, because by the time of the trial he was dead, it was the trial for his murder   Yes, I'll begin again. When the maid came back   From Buenos Aires, because my mother asked her to, I realized that we

were running the risk of her seeing us   No, not my mother, her room was far away, the maid! because she hated the boy. I told him that I was afraid, but he kept coming to see me. The maid heard noises one night but she didn't catch on, but another night she heard the same noises and went out to the courtyard. Then she caught sight of him jumping over the wall on his way back to the police station and heard the slight noise of my window closing   Yes, by then it was winter   She caught on this time and the next night she stayed in the courtyard, with the terrible cold outside, waiting for him to leave my room   He would go before it was light out. I had fallen asleep that fatal night, he woke me up when he was ready to jump from the window to the garden, so that I'd close the window. It was that famous winter of '39, that was so cold. I was settling down to go back to sleep again when I heard some horrible screams of pain. I jumped out of bed and opened the window. You couldn't hear anything by then, the maid had had the nerve to wait for him and she had stabbed him twice   Yes, I called papa and mama, I naturally was afraid that the maid would come and kill me   But I saw papa go over to where she was, kneeling next to him lying there dead, with the kitchen knife in his heart. She didn't move, papa went over to her and asked her to pull the knife out and give it to him. She obeyed him and papa without dirtying his hands picked up the knife by the blade with two fingers and took her by the arm into the house. Mama asked her what she had done and the maid was kind of stupefied, she didn't react to anything. Mama asked me to bring perfume and alcohol for her to smell. I was scared stiff that papa and mama would realize what had happened. In the bathroom I saw the little bottle of sleeping pills, Luminal. I grabbed two pills and hid them in my fist. I came back and told mama I couldn't find them, because my mother really does have the habit of

189

putting everything away and sometimes I don't find things, so then she went to look for the perfume and alcohol. And I put the pills in the maid's mouth and made her swallow them. But they got stuck in her throat, mama came back and gave her a glass of water but she didn't realize what it was, and my mama is no fool. A few minutes later the maid was asleep. When the police asked me what had happened I got up the nerve God knows how . . . and I lied to them. I told them the boy tried to take advantage of the maid and that she defended herself with the kitchen knife. Ay, Father! I had imagined all that more than once, I had already imagined it could happen, and he didn't pay any attention to me   No, the maid didn't wake up until the next morning, I spent the whole night by her side, and I was so insistent that the doctor didn't let them take her to the police station, and so they left a sergeant on watch who went to the kitchen from time to time to eat. Because I don't know if you've noticed, but policemen and doctors are so accustomed to misfortunes that they don't lose their calm. And priests, excuse me for saying this, but I do think you also control yourselves a lot. When the poor wretch woke up I told her that if she told the truth they would condemn her to life imprisonment and she would never see her son again. I explained it till she understood that she wasn't to say anything about the boy being in my room, that he had jumped over the wall to see her, to take advantage of her again, and that it was no longer worth the trouble to get back at me, the main thing was to save herself so that she'd be able to give her baby all the comforts—a manner of speech—and I explained very clearly to her what she had to put in her statement. She looked at me without saying a word. And everything came out fine. She understood that she had to lie for them to let her go. And everybody believed it was in legitimate defense. The only ones who knew the truth were the

maid, the lawyer, and myself, and of course the dead
boy   The one that died   What sick boy? No,
the one I left hasn't died, he still lives, the poor fellow,
I'm saying the other one   The one the maid
killed!   No, Father, what good would that do?
         But what for if the poor wretch did it out of
pure ignorance?   You think that God hasn't forgiven
her?   And doesn't God have another way of punish-
ing her?   does Justice have to necessarily punish
her?   Yes, Father, you're right, the truth has to be
known   Okay, Father, I promise, I'll tell the whole
truth, who should I see?   I don't remember the
judge's name   I don't think he died from the first
stab, from the second   God forgives everything for
just one second of repentance?   Then I'll do it,
Father, that way his sufferings in Purgatory will be
shortened   Father, do you think he had that second of
repentance? because if he didn't he must have gone to hell
and there nobody can help him no matter how much we living pray   What?   But what can I do for
him?   Yes, they're very poor   He must be
three or four years old   Yes, in those shack districts
they become thieves, riffraff   You mean when he
reaches school age?   Yes, I promise   As long
as I can?   Yes, Father, I promise both things: I'll go
and tell the whole truth and I'll take charge of that poor little
thing's education   Yes, Father, I repent   For
everything   Ten Lord's Prayers and ten Ave Marias,
and two Rosaries every night   Yes, Father, I realize
it, I know I am weak   But what fault of mine was it if
I didn't love him anymore?   Should I have married a
sick boy if I didn't love him? isn't it a sin to marry a man
without being in love with him? isn't it deceiving him? isn't
deceiving a sin?   Yes, I'm convinced   Thanks,

Father, I promise   In the name of the Father, the Son, and the Holy Ghost. Amen.

Saturday, April 18, 1947, at 3:00 P.M., Juan Carlos Jacinto Eusebio Etchepare ceased to exist. Beside him were his mother and his sister, whom he had come to visit for Easter as he did every year, since the beginning of autumn was the period recommended by the doctors for his brief stays in Vallejos. He had not left his room during the last four days due to a profound physical exhaustion. At noon he had eaten with more appetite than usual, but a sharp pain in his chest woke him from his siesta, he cried out loud for his mother and a few moments later he stopped breathing, asphyxiated by a pulmonary hemorrhage. Dr. Malbrán arrived ten minutes later and pronounced him dead.

The aforementioned Saturday, April 18, 1947, at 3:00 P.M., Nélida Enriqueta Massa née Fernández scrubbed the kitchen floor of her apartment in Buenos Aires with a wet rag. She had finished washing the lunch dishes and utensils and she was satisfied at having gotten her way, despite her husband's opposition. He had complained again about the maid not working Saturdays and had asked his wife to leave the dishwashing for after siesta. Nené had replied that the cold congealed grease would be much harder to remove and he, sullenly, had continued to argue saying that her entrance into the bedroom later on would awaken him and he would not be able to obtain the sleep he so much needed to calm his nerves. Nené had finally answered that to avoid annoying him she would lie down on one of the children's beds after finishing with the kitchen.

The aforementioned Saturday, April 18, 1947, at 3:00 P.M., María Mabel Catalano née Sáenz, taking advantage of her mother's presence in Buenos Aires to celebrate Easter together, left her in charge of washing the kitchen and took her two-year-old daughter out for some sunshine in the square. The men's shop on the corner was not open, as she had already feared, so it would not be possible to see the young salesman with whom she was on such friendly terms.

The aforementioned Saturday, April 18, 1947, at 3:00 P.M., the mortal remains of Francisco Catalino Páez lay in the common grave at the Vallejos cemetery. Only his skeleton remained and it was covered by other corpses in varying stages of decomposition, the most recent of which still retained the linen in which they were wrapped before being thrown into the mouth of the pit. This was covered by a wooden lid which the visitors to the cemetery, particularly the children, would usually remove to observe the inside. The linen would gradually disintegrate in contact with the putrid matter and after a while the bare bones would remain exposed. The common grave was located at the back of the cemetery beyond the poorer dirt tombs; a tin sign indicated the ossuary and different types of weeds grew around it. The cemetery, far from the rest of town, had the form of a rectangle and cypress trees lined it on all sides. The nearest fig tree could be found on a farm situated a little less than a mile away, and given the time of year, it was laden with ripe fruit.

The aforementioned Saturday, April 18, 1947, at 3:00 P.M., Antonia Josefa Ramírez decided to kill the red chicken in the henhouse because the Leghorn chicken which she had already set apart in a corner of the yard, its legs tied, was a little thin and the customer had ordered a particularly meaty one. She asked a barefoot, seven-year-old girl to run after him and catch him. She was the youngest daughter of the widower with whom she had been living in concubinage for nearly two years, that is, her aunt's next-door neighbor. Fanny didn't want to interrupt his eldest son, of twelve years of age, who was hoeing the garden, and the other two middle children, eleven and nine years old, were working in town as delivery boys, in a grocery store and at an inn respectively. Her own son, Francisco Ramírez, was nine years old and he worked as a newspaper boy. Therefore Fanny had to use the youngest girl, since advanced pregnancy prevented her from running after the animals in the yard.

*

The box which contained the remains of Juan Carlos Jacinto Eusebio Etchepare was placed in a niche in the new white wall built months before, a few steps from the main entrance of the Vallejos cemetery. The wall consisted of four horizontal rows of niches and the box was placed in the third row, priced highest since the inscriptions were at the eye level of those who visited the place. Few niches were occupied.

The white marble slab was adorned by two glass flower vases, each sustained by bronze arms screwed into the marble. The inscriptions designating the deceased's name and dates of birth and death were engraved in bas-relief, and four bronze memorial plaques, in different designs, appeared somewhat squeezed together, owing to the limited space available.

The plaque placed in the upper left-hand corner had the form of an open book placed over mistletoe branches and from its pages undulating letters stood out in high relief:

"JUAN CARLOS! FRIENDSHIP was the motto of your life. This homage of pure affection goes with you to

your last dwelling place. For your great camarade-
rie you will never fade from the memory of your
classmates of P.S. 1 and we hope that the immense
misfortune of having lost you will not make us forget the great fortune of having known you. . . .
Your memory is a rosary of beads that begins and
ends in infinity."

The plaque placed in the upper right-hand corner had a
rectangular shape. Beside a torch in relief the following inscription was set down in straight parallel lines:

"JUAN CARLOS J. E. ETCHEPARE R.I.P. Demised 4-18-
1947. This life is a dream, the true awakening is
death, in whose presence we are all equal. Your su-
periors, comrades, and friends at the mayor's office,
in your memory."

The plaque placed in the lower left-hand corner was
square and had as its sole adornment a cross:

"JUANCA! with your departure I have lost not only
my dear brother, but the best friend of my now im-
poverished existence. Your unforgettable memory
builds a temple in my heart that will perennially receive the incense of my tears. . . . Eternally from
the beyond may your good soul be your little sister's guiding light GOD'S WILL BE DONE   CELINA."

The remaining plaque, placed in the lower right-hand
corner, consisted of an angel with his eyes closed and his arms
crossed over his chest, suspended on a cloud onto which rays
fall from above. The inscription said:

"Quiet!   my little boy sleeps   Mama."

*

. . . he always looked at me when I went by the bar, on
my way home from running errands. . . . Hail Mary, full of
grace, God is with thee, blessed art Thou amongst women
and blessed is the fruit of thy womb, Jesus. Holy Mary,

Mother of God, pray for us sinners now and in the hour of our death, amen. . . . For it to rain so the grass won't dry, for my grandmother to get better, for the locusts who eat the whole crop not to come back anymore, for there not to be anymore locust swarms, at the age of thirteen, Holy Mary Mother of God, what did I know about men! and from that day on I wished he would die, and now I ask forgiveness with all my heart for having wished death upon that poor boy who died yesterday, whom I hated so much, so many years ago! September 14, 1937, already nine years ago, mama, and there's something I never told you, but promise me you'll be kind to me after I tell you, something I could never tell anybody! he always looked at me when I went by the bar, and today above all I ask for my family's health, for the rain to fall on the fruit trees, for the seeds to bud, for the harvest to give us a little more this year than last, after running errands, mama, you know, when I'd pass the bar if he didn't notice I'd look at him but one day he wasn't there anymore and I don't know how many months went by when the girl next door saw him come off the express bus with a tan! where had he been for such a long time? . . . at five o'clock it's nighttime in the winter, on a dark street a block from the bar, could he be following me? "You're from the farm on the other side of the tracks, right? you're a young lady already" and he began to talk to me . . . that he had been vacationing on a ranch, you know, mama, he had come back the day before on the express bus and was very bitter he told me, because he had suffered a great disappointment . . . on the corner near home, at the open fields, he told me about the spring dance, and that he was sure I'd be Miss Spring when I was fifteen, so very bitter he was that night, he had had an argument with Nené, remember her, mama? she was a packer at the Argentine Bargain Store, she hasn't lived here for many years now. "How bitter I am," that boy said to me, and I don't remember anything else, was I on fire? drunk? asleep? he had a kind look about him, mama, don't you remember? I was thirteen, when I came in you were angry because I had taken so long, I peeled the potatoes for you as fast as I could, and I chopped the onion, peeled the garlic, cut it into little pieces, you looked at me, mama, don't you remember that I came in trembling? because I had run a little since it was late, it was the lie I told, mama, and what if it makes my mama sad when I tell her everything? that boy who took advantage of me died, do you understand, mama? he did to me the worst thing that a boy can do to a girl, he took my honor away forever, you won't believe me? Before all I pray to heaven for the health of my whole family, and if I can get by without saying anything to mama it would be much better, and at five the next day I went by again to ask him many things . . . if he was still really mad at Nené . . . but he didn't say hello to me, he didn't follow me and never again did he speak to me, mama, only one time did he walk by my side! because he had gotten what he wanted, the wretch, so let him die! . . . Holy Virgin of Virgins, I did wish him death, and could someone have heard me? . . . I want to remove this sin from me, it wasn't his fault, it was I who let myself be tempted, please don't let it be my fault that this boy died! mama, I'm not going to tell you anything, what for? you'll get bitter like me, if God helps me I'll keep my mouth shut. What was the matter with the boy that day? "How bitter I am," he said to me walking by my side, but after that day he never spoke to me again. . . .

God of my soul, help me in this moment, my little son has left me, and I just can't stand the grief any longer, I too am going to die, and I beg you to let him into your kingdom, because he didn't have time to confess, and he must be laden with sins, but listen to me, dear God, because I'm going to pray to you until I die, and to the Most Holy Mother of God, the Good Virgin Mary, who knows the grief of losing a young son, and my son was no saint like yours, Mother of Jesus, but he wasn't bad, I always told him to go to Mass, to take communion, and the worst part is that he was so . . . boyish, he only wanted to have fun all the time, to go out with the girls, it's their fault more than his, Blessed Virgin, we both are women, we can't condemn a boy because he's like that, men are like that, isn't it true? it's the bad women who are to blame . . . and it's impossible for me to know, but God who's in Heaven and sees everything must know the truth about that money, Blessed Lady of Mount Carmel, and you being the patron saint of this church, help me in this moment, because I'm afraid my son might not be resting, he might be suffering, because of the money he took from that miserable mayor's office, and he never confessed after that, I hope to God he confessed in Córdoba some time, but I asked him and he . . . because he's such a child . . . told me he didn't. Is it because he just wouldn't admit it? there are so many pretty chapels in Córdoba my boy told me, he must have gone to one of them to pray and ask forgiveness, but just so he wouldn't give me the satisfaction, he lied, that he had never entered a church again, and I'm afraid that God might not want him for being a thief, when the truth is that some bad woman must have been tempting him to do that, anyway his sister returned it all bit by bit, so if you rob and then return something, is it still a sin? Blessed Lady of Mount Carmel, speak to Our Lord and explain that my poor dear son was blinded by his anger at their not giving him leave and he took advantage of an unwatched moment to take that money, filthy pesos, for sure some woman asked him for that money. . . . Blessed Virgin of Mount Carmel, I don't know if you've been a mother too, like the Virgin Mary, because then you'd know what I'm suffering, from thinking that in this moment something bad is happening to him, he suffered so much already in this world, with the cough and the choking, dear Virgin, does he have to keep suffering in the next world too?

God Almighty Father, Creator of the Heaven and the Earth, I pray that my deceased husband be resting. I loved him truly but he left me such a long time ago, to let me suffer so many disappointments since then, Lord, how different my life would have been if he hadn't left me alone. But that was your will, so that perhaps by suffering I would value all that I lost, and that's for sure, a good man like him is hard to come by. He is surely in your kingdom of glory, I beg of you also to remember to make my daughter a good wife and mother, she's very good and may she never stop being so, she turned out good like her father, and my two dear grandsons, let them grow healthy and good, I pray to you for this every day. I don't ask anything for myself, if the boardinghouse is sold, let it be sold, I don't care, if it's auctioned away let it be, I'm tired of the mountains anyway, all I ask for is health, so I can work and so I won't be a burden to my daughter, I don't want her to find out that I'm stonebroke. . . . I ask only for my health, and if they auction away my boarding-house let me have something left after I pay the mortgage, so that I can give it to my kid, she should get something out of the little her father left. . . . I'm ashamed to ask for something else, for that poor boy, who I lived in sin with, and who is now no more. I forgive him, dear God, he was a scatter-brain, I don't want to hold a grudge against him, he's dead now, he can't do anybody any more harm now, and I'm not complaining, I'm going to take what's coming to me, if I goofed I'm going to take what's coming to me, because it's the punishment I deserve. Because one thing is to let what was mine go to seed, but what was my kid's, that's a different story. If I knew he didn't have a head for money, why did I listen to him and mortgage what was my kid's as well? I don't ask anything for me, just health, so I won't be a burden to my son-in-law, so I can do work, any kind. I only ask for my daughter to be well, and for her children, and for that poor boy to be resting, because I don't hold any grudge against him, really.

Our Father, who art in Heaven, hallowed be Thy name, Thy kingdom come, Thy will be done, on earth as it is in heaven. Give us this day our daily bread. And forgive us our trespasses as we forgive those who trespass against us. And lead us not into temptation, but deliver us from evil. Amen. But I can't resign myself, I can't, Jesus, because none of it was his fault, others were to blame, my brother was good, and now we're alone, mama and I, and when sickness is brought on by the hand of fate it's different, but when it's brought on because someone provokes it then I cannot resign myself: if she hadn't kept tempting him . . . this wouldn't have happened. Jesus Christ, let there be justice, let that woman get her just deserts, a sickly boy, with a cold, and she made him stand at that gate hours and hours, till morning, she made him stay with her wicked wiles! I ask that that woman get her just deserts, soon, because if not I won't be able to go on living, out of my hate for her, and also I'm sure she was the one he stole for at the mayor's office, she must have asked him to! so that they could elope, that's why they must have pretended to break up, but don't ever let her cross my path, God forbid! because I won't be responsible for my acts, I don't want to know where she is, or if she's dead or alive! just don't let her cross my path because if she does I'll tear her to pieces. . . .

FIFTEENTH EPISODE

She was one of the dreaded Cat People
—doomed to slink and prowl by night . . .
fearing always that a lover's kiss might
change her into a snarling, clawing killer!

(ad for *Cat People*, starring
Simone Simon and Kent Smith)

Vallejos, August 21, 1947

Dear Nené:

I hope these lines find you in the best of health. Before anything let me apologize for having taken so long in answering your letters, but you can well imagine the reason, when it concerns someone of my years. Aches and pains, my dear, that keep me more and more from doing what I want.

What happened is that I had a slight cold and I couldn't go to the post office, and I don't dare trust anybody, so that I didn't take your letters out of the box until a few days ago, I have to watch out for Celina so that she won't be suspicious. And it grieves me to know that you too are mortified by the dear boy's passing away with the guilty one still alive, but I believe that we should leave it to destiny to give that wanton woman her deserts, let us not think any further about who it could have been, why unmask her? the evil is done.

The best thing is to write to each other and to talk about ourselves and become closer and closer. About myself, my dear, what can I tell you, my life is over, only friends like you who are so kind as to remember me are of any comfort, and for remembering Juan Carlos too, God bless him and keep him.

In your most recent letter you seem a little offended, but by now you must realize that if I didn't write you it was for reasons of health. I do hope that your marital life improves, what's going on between you two? Maybe with my experience I can give you advice. I think that a woman can be happy even beside a man she doesn't love, as long as she knows how to understand and to forgive. Does he have a really bad defect? I'm referring to defects in character. That sadness comes over me too in the late afternoons, those hours never pass! between four and eight, from when it starts getting dark until dinner time, I get through it somehow trying to find little things to do, some darning, some light sewing. And don't your kids make your life happier? have they been a disappointment in some way?

Forgive me for being such a busybody, but since I'm becoming fond of you I feel like I want to know more about your life, so that I can help you although it be through my prayers only.

Also please forgive me for having made you wait for my reply. Do write soon.

Affectionately,
Leonor Saldívar de Etchepare

Postscript: I forgot to thank you for reminding me of Juan Carlos's wish to be cremated. We must leave aside all selfishness and do his bidding, even though it is not in agreement with our beliefs, isn't that so?

Before addressing the envelope she looks at her mother, knitting in a chair several yards away. The rhythm of the knitting is sustained, it does not indicate fatigue, which leads the daughter to think that the old woman will stay seated a while longer. She hurriedly writes the envelope before she can be discovered and leaves the house in the direction of the post office after telling her mother that she is going to the drugstore.

*

Vallejos, September 10, 1947

Dearest Nené:

What joy it gave me to receive your sweet little letter! I am so happy to know that you forgive my delay in writing to you and I thank you for having the confidence in me to tell me your problems: I too need someone I can trust in, Nené, because my daughter worries me a great deal. You see, a young doctor from Buenos Aires, Dr. Marengo, has come here to work at the new hospital, he's a very nice boy with a great future, and all the girls chase after him he's so good-looking, and, well, the other day he came to ask me for Celina's hand in marriage. But he's a stranger, and I was so worried that I asked him for a few months' time, at least till the mourning period is over, so that I can have time to decide. Celina is very obedient and she accepted my conditions. Do you think I did right? I hope he's a nice boy, because then Celina will marry one of the best catches in town.

Please don't suffer because of Juan Carlos's cremation, if it goes through we will let you know at the proper moment. It was his will and one must respect it, no matter whose wishes it goes against. I know that you're having a hard time of it now, how tough it is to be the mother of boys! But you don't tell me anything about your husband, you never even mention his name, is something unpleasant happening? you know that you can trust me.

In my last letter I forgot to tell you that I am looking for and classifying all of Juan Carlos's letters that I can find, so feel easy: I shall send them to you very soon.

Now I'm going to ask you a favor, could you give me your husband's office address, if you could be so kind, because a Mrs. Piaggio here is coming to Buenos Aires soon and wants to buy a lot, and I told her that your husband was an auctioneer. It would be such a comfort for her to deal with an acquaintance. Thank you so much for your help.

Nothing else to say right now so I'll take my leave of you till next time. I look forward to hearing from you especially since it seems that my daughter will leave home soon, could I have found in you another daughter? Tell me also what you think of her possible marriage (they don't even want to worry about engagements) to that boy. Despite the fact that you're not on speaking terms with Celina, I know you have a good heart and that you'll be glad, right? imagine, married to a doctor! What all the girls dream of.

Yours most affectionately,
Leonor Saldívar de Etchepare

Dressed only in her nightgown, she has become chilled while writing. She shivers. She thinks of her brother's illness, begun with a cold. Her mother sleeps in the next bed. She hides the envelope inside one of the homework folders belonging to her pupils. She lies down in bed and gropes for the hot-water bottle with her feet. She decides that she will pass the post office and mail the letter the next day, on her way back from school.

*

Vallejos, September 26, 1947

Sir:

I'm sending you these letters so that you'll know who your wife is. She did me a great wrong and I'm not going to let her do it to you or to anybody, not without receiving the punishment she deserves.

It won't interest you to know who I am, though it may be easy for you to guess. She thinks she's going to get her way all the time, somebody has to show her in her true colors.

Respectfully yours,
A true friend

The door is locked, the running cold water from the faucet covers all sounds. Seated on the edge of the bathtub she then writes the address on the large envelope: "Mr. Donato José Massa, B.A.S.I. Real Estate, Sarmiento 873 4th fl., Buenos Aires." She takes two letters with the salutation "Dearest Mrs. Etchepare" and signed "Nené." In the first letter she underlines the following paragraph:

"Sometimes with my kids, listening to all the innocent nonsense they say, one realizes things that one never thought about. The baby is always pestering me and his brother with questions, he asks what animal we like the best, and which house we like the best, and which car, and whether the machine gun or the revolver or the rifle, and suddenly the other day he said to me (since we were alone because the flu is going around school and he stayed home with a cold), 'Mommy, what do you like best in the whole world?' and I immediately thought of one thing, but of course I couldn't say it: Juan Carlos's face. Because in my whole life I've never seen anything as lovely as Juan Carlos's face, may he rest in peace. And my kids, they aren't much to look at, as babies they were adorable but now they have little eyes, fleshy noses, they look more and more like their father, and seeing them so ugly makes me feel that I don't love them. When I see a mother with a handsome child on the street it makes me mad. . . . I feel better when my kids walk in front of me, I feel ashamed sometimes that they've turned out that way."

In the second letter she underlines the following:

". . . and as soon as I hear his footsteps in the hallway I want to die. Everything I do is wrong as far as he's concerned, and what does he have that's so perfect? I don't know what's the matter with him, he must realize I don't love him and that's why he's so mean to me. . . . But Mrs. Etchepare, I swear, I do the best I can to hide the disgust I feel toward him, but of course when he gets nasty with me and the kids, then I wish he were dead. I don't know how God decides who's to die and who's to keep on living. And it was your son's turn to die, how you must suffer.

"Is it possible that when you ask for something, you don't get it if you tell someone else about it? All the same I'm going to tell you, because in the end it's as if we were one and the same. Well, it so happens that every time the kids see a lady bug they say 'lady bug, lady bug, bring me luck' and they whisper two wishes, and yesterday on my way back from the market I saw a lady bug and asked for two things, do you think God won't give them to me if I tell you? Well, first I asked that in the next world, if God forgives me after the Last Judgment, because I'm sure he forgives Juan Carlos, then could I be reunited with him in the other life. And the second thing I asked is for my kids to get handsomer as they grow up because that way I can love them more, I don't say they should be handsome like Juan Carlos but just not as ugly as their father. He wasn't so ugly when we were first married, but with the years besides he got so much fatter that you can't recognize him. But you never know how the kids will turn out when they grow up, no? you can't be sure.

"If you were only closer so that we could unburden ourselves together. The only thing that comforts me is that one day everything's going to come to an end because I'm going to die, because I can be sure of that, right? one fine day everything's going to come to an end because I'm going to die."

She folds the two letters again and together with the one she herself wrote, puts them into the aforementioned large envelope. She takes another envelope of the same size and writes the address: Mrs. Nélida Fernández de Massa, Olleros 4328 apt. 2B, Buenos Aires. She takes six letters with the salutation "My Dear," and the signature "Juan Carlos." She puts them into the second envelope and considers her task finished. She comes out of the bathroom with both envelopes hidden between her chest and her bathrobe.

—Why did you take so long?

—I was tweezing my eyebrows. You only have the sleeves left to knit now?

—Yes, turn on the heater, child. I'm cold.

—It's spring already, mama.

—What do I care about the calendar! I'm cold.

—Mama, I found out something . . . that made me very happy.

—What was it?

—They told me that creepy Nené is having trouble with her husband.

—Who told you?

—Gossip needs no carriage.

—Child, don't be like that, tell me.

—No, they made me swear not to say a word, be satisfied with what I've told you.

—And I wonder how she's doing, do you think she knows Juan Carlos passed away?

—Yes, mama, she must know.

—She could have sent us a condolence card, Mabel did. Maybe it's because she has a lot of work with the kids, how many does she have? two?

—Yes, mama, two boys.

—She'll never be alone, then. She'll always have a man in the house. . . . I don't understand how Nené's mother can stay here in Vallejos when she has two grandsons in Buenos Aires. If you had married it would have been different . . .

—Now, mama, don't begin again. I have to tell you something, but don't get angry at me.

—I won't get angry at you, tell me.

—Nené did send condolences, but I didn't show it to you, I didn't want to remind you of the things of the past.

—So she remembered, poor thing.

—Yes, mama, she remembered.

—Ay . . . if I had grandchildren I wouldn't be the way I am . . . God took my son and I hope my daughter isn't going to stay single on me, if I die you know very well what my worry will be . . .

—Mama . . .

—Yes, mama, mama, you have to be more on your toes with the boys, you know so many and all of them are only friends. Flirt with them a little.

—But if they don't like me what am I to do . . .

—And that Doctor Marengo? didn't you tell me that he asks you to dance all the time?

—Yes, but as a friend.

—Dear, I've been told that you have been seen in his car, why didn't you tell me?

—Oh, it was nothing, a few days before Juan Carlos passed away. I think it was raining, and he drove me home after the novena services.

—I'd like to meet him, they say he's very nice.

—Yes, mama, but he's engaged to be married, his fiancée is in Buenos Aires. . . .

—Dear, why do you get like this?

—Because mama, you drive me up the wall.

—So nervous, such a young girl and so nervous.

—I'm not such a young girl anymore, can't you shut up!

—Come, dear, don't get angry at me. . . . Don't lock yourself in the room again . . .

—Hello, they sent me here from the San Roque Hostel, is this where Mr. Juan Carlos Etchepare lived?

—Yes, what can I do for you?

—Why, don't I know you from somewhere?

—I don't know. . . . Who are you?

—Mrs. Massa, and these are my two children.

—You're Nené. Don't you remember me?

—It can't be . . . Elsa DiCarlo . . .

—Yes, I own the boardinghouse. Are you staying in Cosquín for a few days?

—We don't know . . . I don't think so . . . we left the suitcases at the bus station.

—I have a room with two beds, but have a seat, Mrs. Massa. How did you find the house?

—The hostel sent me, I went there and asked them where Juan Carlos had lived these last years.

—Look, Mrs. Massa, if you want I'll put another little bed in that room and the three of you can be comfortable, your husband is not coming with you?

—No, he stayed in Buenos Aires. But I think we'll continue on to La Falda, today, is there a bus?

—Yes, but you're going to have to hurry. It's in a half-hour.

—Yes, I better take it.

—What adorable kids, I can see you have everything in life, but don't they go to school? are you staying for a while?

—Children, play in the courtyard for a while, I have to speak to the lady.

—You probably know that Juan Carlos died in Vallejos. He left here at the end of March to spend a few days with his family, and he didn't come back. . . .

—Yes, I know, he's been dead half a year already. And have you been here a long time?

—Yes, a few years, I set up this boardinghouse and he came to live here. The family was sending him very little and if it was enough to pay for room and board, it wasn't enough for treatment. That's why I set up a boardinghouse, but I never imagined what I was getting myself into. Your work is never through at a boardinghouse. . . . But how strange, having your vacation in October, it was a smart move, there are very few people here now, and it's neither too hot nor too cold.

—Did Juan Carlos remember me?

—Yes, he mentioned you sometimes.

— . . . And did he love you?

—Don't ask me such questions, Nené.

—You know that I loved him with all my heart, don't you?

—Yes, but nobody has a right to ask me anything, I earn my living and don't ask anybody for anything. And you're a married woman who has everything, so now you know. I don't want to talk about Juan Carlos, may he rest in peace.

—I'm not a married woman anymore. My husband and I separated, that's why I came here.

—I didn't know . . . and why did you come here?

—Juan Carlos always talked about Cosquín in his letters, I wanted to see it, and to talk to someone who could tell me things about him.

—He had gotten very thin, Nené. And he was always the same Juan Carlos, going to the bar all the time, and toward the end he gave me a lot of headaches, although it's wrong to say. . . . He gambled a lot, toward the end it was the only thing that distracted him, but you don't know how I have to sweat and slave in this boardinghouse, I have to be everywhere, Nené, if not, the cook spends too much on me, and I have to do the cleaning and the shopping and I really have to be everywhere at once. That's the only way to get a little profit out of having a boardinghouse. You probably find me aged, don't you?

—Well, it's been many years.

—But how sorry I am about your husband . . . what happened? can't you tell me?

—These things happen. . . . It was only two weeks ago, just a short while, that's why I came here. But he's the one who deserted the home, so I don't have anything to worry about.

—Was there another woman?

—No, but he realized that everything had ended between us. Now he's sorry and came to say good-by to us at the train, but I think it's better this way. Even though the kids lose a few days of school it was better to come here because if not I would have felt sorry for him and given in again.

—And the kids? aren't they going to miss their father?

—It's worse for them to see us fighting like cats and dogs the whole day long.

—You must know what you're doing.

—The only man I ever loved in my whole life was Juan Carlos.

—The last year especially, he suffered a lot, the poor boy. . . . I had to get up at night to change his sheets, soaked through with sweat, and to give him a clean change, and food, constantly, he'd get hungry any time of the day, and then leave half of it on the plate. But here the biggest headache is the maids, the mountain girls are so unreliable, and what I needed more than anything was the washerwoman because with all those bedclothes that had to be changed I never had enough sheets, Nené, and to leave him with the same sheets made me feel bad. There were spells when I'd be changing his sheets all day long. Want me to show you his room? He had his room apart, with a little bed, would you like to see it?

—Yes . . .

—And he often mentioned you, Nené.

—And who else did he mention?

—Mabel. He mentioned her often too.

—Really?

—But he didn't love her at all, he said she was selfish. While he always spoke well of you, he said you were the only one he thought of marrying, I'm telling you this without any jealousy on my part, Nené, life is full of twists, isn't it?

—And what else did he say about me?

—Well, just that, that you were a good girl, and that at one time he was going to marry you.

—And you don't know if he wanted to see me, toward the end? as a friend I mean . . .

—Well . . . the truth is I'd get mad when he talked about girls, so that there are many things he didn't tell me. . . . Come see the room now, you'll have to go to the station pretty soon or you'll miss the bus.

—I don't know if I should go or stay. . . .

—No, you'd better go, Nené, see what a pretty white

room? that was his bed, don't you think it's better not to stir up old memories? Don't take me wrong . . .

—Did he stay in his room a lot?

—When he felt sick. . . . Mister Teodoro! stop a second. . . . Look Nené, the taxi's just passing by, you want to take it?

—Well . . .

—I must look like I've aged, right, Nené?

—Well, the years pass for everyone.

—Just a moment, Mister Teodoro!

—Children, come, it's late.

—You're in luck, there are so few taxis here.

—Mrs. DiCarlo . . . I feel like staying . . .

—No, you better not, Nené, I don't want to talk about the old days anymore, I want to forget all that.

—I wish you could have told me more . . .

—No, look, I'm a very bitter person, now why should I make you bitter too? . . . Just a minute, Mister Teodoro, here comes the lady . . . you have to take her to the bus station, quickly . . .

. . . "While he always spoke well of you, saying you were the only one he thought of marrying" . . . oh my Lord who art in Heaven, this my prayer you have heard, promise me you won't forget, LA FALDA 25 MILES I'm traveling this road to nowhere, where can it be I'm going? nowhere . . . "And what else did he say about me? . . ." "Well, just that, that you were a good girl, and that at one time he meant to marry you" . . . me? of course, me! because he couldn't ignore this heart that I have put before him, DRIVE SLOWLY CURVE 165 FEET but the heart, who drives the heart? because without any warning we'll hear trumpets far away, then marimba rhythms will die away, no more dancing no more sway,

CÓRDOBA'S FINEST! LA SERRANITA MINERAL WATER heaven's finest? this very minute the angels will appear, where is it they're taking me to? the earth is already below as our souls fly higher toward the sun, beneath me the ocean still hugs the shore, but fear grows since the sun shines no more, will the blue of the night meet the gold of the day? Again those trumpets call far away, do they proclaim that she who loved on earth has nothing to fear for her beloved? but the darkness of space is infinite and the angels are beside me no longer . . . MARZOTTO WINE, ARGENTINA'S FAVORITE and whose favorite am I? will I be so in death if I was not in life? people pass away, down below they stay, my family too now is dead, their stiff bodies forsaken, he who would pinch himself and from some dream awaken, vainly would he try to touch his flesh, for now all flesh has faded . . . into thin air! But my dreams too have faded like an unfinished melody, while God looks down and laughs at what a romantic girl I still be DRIVE SLOWLY, CURVE 265 FEET why slow down? if I'm a fool then it's a fool I want to be, don't pity me! nor laugh at me! Is Juan Carlos near or far away? through these black clouds one can see a grave, a white cemetery that I think I know . . . it's pampas soil I recognize . . . and little wild flowers that once I used to gather, by what strange command have I been brought here? can this one be Vallejos's cemetery? my father is standing beside a shabby tombstone but to me he does not cry out "perfidious," and kissing my forehead he has already left me, arm in arm he and my mother are going, but can what I see now be real? the dust their steps raise, do the dead put back their carnal cloak? where am I? who am I? has God absolved my soul of all burdens and guilt? One day I woke and saw him wander by, then simply ignoring that it came from me I softly sighed "do take me!" and ever since my heart hasn't been my own, a deeper sadness I have never known, and still I cry "do take me!"

Juan Carlos, I really mean it, ask God if I ever forgot you . . . life, with it's dirty dishes and diapers and another's kisses that I should have spurned, did life try that way to suppress my yearning? ha, ha . . . and you, where will I find you, moonlight behind you, my one and only love, with somebody else in your arms? are your shining eyes perfidious? forgetful of your sacred vow, are you embracing another's charms? whose charms? is it that old bag you prefer? or maybe it's better she and not another more beautiful than me? Quiet! the world turns pale because, with sure step, he finally reappears . . . and his handsome face reflects an anxious search . . . he looks but cannot find, who is he looking for on these deserted streets? I'm so afraid I hide, where do his firm steps lead? well-dressed women appear, he looks and lets them pass, where can we be? why has he come for me all the way to the store? this uniform is so plain, ah, and this I should have guessed . . . the widow all in black stops him between two counters . . . he looks at her and thanks her for all her sacrifices . . . she tries to block his way . . . he gently but firmly pushes her aside . . . and from behind the counter Celina abruptly appears, and behind her is Mabel all dolled up! . . . why does Mabel stand beside that viper? Celina's hidden and that's why the devils couldn't find her! but wherever she sets her foot the earth starts to tremble, it yawns open wide and high black flames swallow both women! they're gone! dare I look at him now? . . . Beloved one, if you forget me, each day would be a gray day, each tiny hope take wing, my heart be dead . . . that's why I'm trembling, it's not because the sun's going down, although it may turn slightly cold . . . but that leather jacket, why did you wear it today? my father laughed at you . . . "the rancher" he would say . . . now do you see how wrong it was for us to worry? now do you see how in the end we're together? that illness you thought . . . had divided us, was only the detour that united us . . . your sister who hated me . . . today doesn't count, your scornful mother is now far away . . . and that ghastly Nastini, what did he ever matter? that's all behind us . . . in our past life, my husband? he wasn't bad . . . I never loved him, my sons? to God they sing . . . in a choir of angels they make sweet song, my mother? she's gone, and with her my father: they left this humble house to us . . . but what does that look in your eyes mean? you look at me and suddenly the sparks go flying! those devil eyes that know too well the knack of lying . . . now lie no more and take my hand, it's getting cool, the day is dying! . . . do you like these new curtains? I brought them from Buenos Aires . . . and you're right, this gate brings back sweet recollections, but let's go inside and leave the garden, it all began with just a cold so let's be careful, you no longer have it? not even a sniffle? Oh look, in this little room where I lived when I was single . . . here we could start a new life with kisses, a life of love? whatever God wishes! We are before God, Juan Carlos, this is what the catechism proclaimed, this is called the Resurrection, the consequence of Judgment Day, aren't you happy? so this is what they call Resurrection of the Flesh, but am I dreaming? can I awake from my dream without hurting? and if I pinch myself? what? stop all this fear, my fingers touch my flesh and I'm not dreaming since the pinch would have awakened me, God returns us to life in body and soul! it is God's wish, are you ashamed? and the oven's on, mother must have been cooking when she heard the angel's trumpets . . . Juan Carlos! I have a surprise for you . . . in all those years we lived apart . . . I learned to cook! yes! I can make your favorite dish, Juan Carlos, and are you asking me now to lie beside you? to take the most refreshing of all siestas? do you remember asking me to lie in my uniform beside you? you said that in a letter, but what is this tight embrace? what does it mean? is this permitted? Juan Carlos! in this moment I see it clear, I finally realize it! . . . if God made you so handsome it's because He saw your soul was good, and therefore rewarded you, and now kneeling together holding hands, our eyes turned upward, beyond the frills of the new curtains, beside this humble little bed, our love nest? let's ask Our Lord God in this new life, if He will pronounce us, for an eternity, you my man and me your wife . . .

—Mommy, I want to go weewee!

—We'll be there in a minute dear, hold it in.

—Mama, I can't!

—We'll be in La Falda any minute, you can go to the bathroom as soon as we get off. . . . Hold it in a bit more.

—Mommy, I'm bored.

—Look out the window, see how pretty the mountains are, see all the pretty things God created?

Your hands are two shivering doves.

(from H. Manzi's tango "Malena")

Deaths

NÉLIDA ENRIQUETA FERNÁNDEZ DE MASSA, R.I.P., expired on September 15, 1968. Her husband, Donato José Massa, her sons Luis Alberto and Enrique Rubén; her daughter by marriage Mónica Susana Schultz de Massa; her granddaughter María Mónica; her future daughter by marriage Alicia Caracciolo; her father by marriage Luis Massa; her brother and sister by marriage Esteban Francisco Massa and Clara Massa de Iriarte; nephews, nieces, and other kindred invite friends to accompany her mortal remains to the Chacarita cemetery today at 4 P.M.

NÉLIDA ENRIQUETA FERNÁNDEZ DE MASSA, R.I.P., expired on September 15th, 1968. The Massa Realty Co. invites friends to accompany her mortal remains to the Chacarita cemetery today at 4 P.M.

Thursday, September 15, 1968, at 5:00 P.M., Nélida Enriqueta Massa née Fernández ceased to exist, after suffering the vicissitudes of a serious disease. She was fifty-two years of age. She had not left her bed for several months but only during the last days had she surmised her approaching end. The day before her death she received extreme unction, after which she asked to be alone with her husband.

Her eldest son, the medical doctor Luis Alberto Massa,

and her daughter by marriage, who had been tending the sick woman since the tests revealed a cancerous tumor in the spinal column, left the room; son and daughter-in-law accompanied the priest and his acolyte to the door and then went into the kitchen where the two-year-old granddaughter was having a glass of milk and ladyfingers under the watchful eye of the maid. The latter offered them coffee and the couple accepted.

When Nené was alone with her husband, relieved by the morphine but somewhat lethargic, she explained with difficulty that on the occasion of buying the cooperative apartment they had been occupying for the last twelve years, at which time they met with the solicitor to sign certain papers, she had entrusted the latter with an envelope. This contained certain instructions concerning her last will and testament and some letters from thirty years back. The document authorized, first, that she should not be cremated, and second, that the above-mentioned bundle of letters should be placed in the coffin, between the shroud and her breast.

But she wished to change said request, with respect to the letters. She desired that other objects be placed in the coffin, in her hand: a lock of hair from her only granddaughter, the small baby wristwatch that she had given her second son on his first communion, and her husband's engagement ring. He asked her why she was taking his ring, since it would be the only thing he would have left of her. Nené answered that she wanted to take something of his and didn't know why she asked for the ring in particular, but she wanted it, earnestly. Besides, she asked that the letters the solicitor was keeping for her be destroyed, and she wanted her husband to do it, since she was afraid that somebody young and insolent might read them one day and make fun. Her husband promised to satisfy all her requests.

Soon after her second son, civil engineer Enrique

Rubén Massa, entered the room with his betrothed Alicia Caracciolo. Nené repeated her request for the wristwatch before them, fearing that her husband would forget. Then she gradually lost consciousness and asked them to call her mother, dead years back. She did not regain consciousness again.

The aforementioned Thursday, September 15, 1968, at 5:00 P.M., the niche at the Vallejos cemetery where the remains of Juan Carlos Etchepare rested displayed its two customary flower vases, without flowers. The caretaker had recently removed two withered bunches. A new, rectangular, memorial plaque had been added to the old ones, on it a design in relief representing the rising or setting sun over the sea and to one side the following inscription: "JUAN CARLOS   ALL KINDNESS   You left us twenty years ago today   your sister who will never forget you   CELINA 4-18-67." All the other niches in the wall were occupied and at one end of it two more walls had been raised; among others the following names could be read: Antonio Sáenz, Juan José Malbrán, Leonor Saldívar de Etchepare, Benito Jaime García, Laura Pozzi de Baños, Celedonio Gorostiaga.

The aforementioned Thursday, September 15, 1968, at 5:00 P.M., María Mabel Catalano née Sáenz prepared to receive at home the last pupil of the day. Every afternoon, after teaching in the morning at a private school in the Caballito district, she gave individual lessons at home for grammar school children. The bell rang and her twenty-four-year-old daughter, María Laura García Fernández née Catalano, opened the door. A girl pupil walked in, and noticing her teacher's grandson in a corner of the room, asked permission to hold him in her arms. Mabel looked at her two-year-old grandson, Marcelo Juan, metal braces on his left extremities, smiling in the pupil's arms. He had been afflicted with infantile paralysis, and Mabel, despite the retirement pension she received, corresponding to her thirty years as a public school teacher, worked as many hours as she could to help pay the doctor expenses. Her grandson was being treated by the foremost specialists.

The aforementioned Thursday, September 15, 1968, at 5:00 P.M., the mortal remains of Francisco Catalino Páez lay in the common grave at the Vallejos cemetery. Only his skeleton remained and it was covered by other corpses in varying stages of decomposition, the most recent of which still retained the linen in which they were wrapped before being thrown into the mouth of the pit. This was covered by a wooden lid which the visitors to the cemetery, particularly the children, would usually remove to observe the inside. The linen would gradually disintegrate in contact with the putrid matter and after a while the bare bones would remain exposed. The common grave was located at the back of the cemetery beyond the poorer dirt tombs; a tin sign indicated the ossuary and different types of weeds grew around it. The cemetery, far from the rest of town, had the form of a rectangle and cypress trees lined it on all sides. The nearest fig tree could be found on a farm situated a little less than a mile away, and given the time of year, it was covered with light green buds.

The aforementioned Thursday, September 15, 1968, at 5:00 P.M., Antonia Josefa Ramírez, widow of Lodiego, was traveling by chaise from her farm to the business center of Vallejos, nine miles away. Her twenty-one-year-old daughter Ana María Lodiego was going with her. They would visit the stores to continue shopping for the girl's trousseau since she was soon to marry one of their neighbors, the owner of a milk farm. Fanny felt very happy to be going to town, where her four stepsons lived, already the fathers of eleven children who called her grandmother. But her greatest satisfaction lay in visiting her son Pancho, now settled in a newly built cottage. Fanny asked Ana María if it would be better to buy the sheets and towels at the Palomero House or at the Argentine Bargain Store. Her daughter answered that she didn't want to buy something just because it was cheap but because she really liked it, in sheets and towels she didn't want to save money. Fanny thought of Nené the packer, whom she hadn't seen for such a long time, since she had gone to say good-by at the train station, in Buenos Aires, was it thirty years ago? She thought that if Nené had been in Vallejos she would have invited her to her daughter's wedding. Then she thought of Panchito and of the bag of vegetables and the crate of eggs that she was bringing him as a gift. Panchito had a new house and Ana María was about to marry, Fanny thought with satisfaction. That night she would dine at Panchito's house and she wouldn't be considered a burden, because she brought good presents. The chaise shook owing to a rut in the road. Fanny looked at the crate of eggs, her daughter reproached her for having brought so many. Fanny thought that Ana María was jealous of Panchito's house: everything had gone so well since the boy started working in that mechanic's shop. The owner had taken a great liking to him and the owner's daughter had fallen in love with him. Of course Panchito, considered very good-looking among the girls in town for his athletic build and big black eyes, could have married a prettier girl, but the owner's daughter had turned out to be a good housewife. She wasn't pretty, and she had that trouble with her eyes, but none of their three beautiful children had been born cross-eyed like their mother. Panchito's house had been built by his father-in-law in the rear of the lot that was part of the mechanic's shop, which stood next to the side-walk. It had been bound by deed in the couple's name as a wedding gift.

Back in his apartment after meeting with the lawyer, Donato José Massa felt very tired. The house was in dark-ness. The housemaid had left at three in the afternoon as usual and his younger son would not return until later. Despite his insistence, his elder son had refused to remain in the house with his wife and daughter, as they had during the last months of Nené's illness. This first year would be the most difficult to bear, Mr. Massa thought, then his bachelor son would marry and bring his wife to live in that apartment that was too large for two men alone. He turned on an old lamp with a tulle shade and sat on a sofa in the living room. The set of French satin sofas was not protected by the solid brown slipcovers. To avoid wear and tear Nené would take the covers off only on special occasions. Her daughter-in-law had taken them off the night of the wake and had not put them back on. Mr. Massa had an envelope in his hand. He opened it, inside were two groups of letters: a blue ribbon was tied around one group and a pink ribbon around the other. He immediately noticed Nené's handwriting in the pink-ribboned group. . . . He untied the blue ribbon and un-folded one of the letters, but read only a few words. He thought that Nené would doubtlessly disapprove of his inter-ference. He looked at the satin on the sofas, it seemed new and the coffee and liqueur stains from the night of the wake were almost unnoticeable. The house was quiet. He thought that Nené had left an emptiness that no one could fill. He re-membered the two months they had been separated following an unpleasant incident, many years back. He didn't regret having overcome his pride to go and fetch her in Córdoba, where she had taken refuge with their two sons. Standing in front of the incinerator, next to the elevator door, he placed the letters in the envelope and threw them down the black tube.

The letters tied in the pink ribbon fell into the fire and burned without scattering. But the other group of letters, without the blue ribbon to keep them together, curled as they burned and scattered down the incinerator oven. Pages broke loose and the flame that was to blacken and destroy them first illuminated them fleetingly ". . . tomorrow the week is over already . . ." ". . . not to trust blondes, so what are you going to confide to the pillow? . . ." ". . . just a few croco- dile tears . . ."

". . . to the movies? and who's going to buy you chocolate bars, eh . . ." ". . . no dirty tricks because I'll find out . . ."

". . . Kisses till you say stop, Juan Carlos . . ." ". . . here I'm really going to get sick, from getting so worked up about things . . ." ". . . when a bed is vacated it's be- cause one of them died . . ." ". . . I swear, Blondie, I won't ask for more than a kiss . . ." ". . . don't tell anybody, not even your family, that I'm coming back without com- pleting the cure . . ." ". . . I'm making a promise, which is that I'm going to follow all the doctors' directions . . ." ". . . Doll, I'm running out of paper . . ." ". . . because now I feel that I love you very much . . ."

". . . Imagine, Blondie, just from talking to you a little I feel better, how will it be when I see you! . . ." ". . . There's a regular hospital in Cosquín too . . ." ". . . as soon as I have more news I'll write to you again . . ." ". . . the water in the river is nice and warm . . ." ". . . and you too are far away . . ."

". . . but now each time I read your letter I feel confident again . . ."